A Goblin Postman Teen Mystery

Sally Sharp

and the

Corduroy Clue

Patricia Bow

Goblin Postman icon created by Patricia Bow

Cover images:

"Walking Home" by Sarah Joy
(https://www.flickr.com/photos/joybot/7608928956/in/photolist) used by permission, and in accordance with her Creative Commons license.

"Beach" by M R Hayata
(https://www.flickr.com/photos/mrhayata/4598766380/in/set-72157594196970841/) used in accordance with his Creative Commons license.

This book is for

all bright, inquisitive, determined girls:

and especially for Vivian and Eleanor.

Contents

Chapter 1

Girl in Distress

"FOUR O'CLOCK on a Friday," Tasha grumbled as she stepped onto the escalator. "What a time for Fay to want to meet us at the mall! We'll be lucky if we can spot her, let alone get close to her."

"We'll be even luckier if there's three seats left at Jo-Jo's!" Sally squeezed in beside her friend and looked back to watch the panorama that opened below them as the escalator slid slowly upward. The mall was a sea of bodies, a lot of them teens lured in by the pre-school-opening sales. The babble of voices drowned out even the Muzak.

Outside the refrigerated shopping centre, the August afternoon was thick with the humid heat that promised a thunderstorm. And played havoc with hair. Tasha pushed back a mass of frizzing chestnut curls that kept falling into her eyes.

Sally used the spare seconds on the escalator to twist her long dark-blond hair into a knot behind her head and secure it with a scrunchy. "So she's got some fantastic news, eh? I wonder what it could be?"

Tasha laughed. "Any bets it's some cool new boy she's met?"

An uproar broke out at the top of the escalator. They heard a girl's protesting voice, then hoots of laughter. From the top downward, like a row of dominoes tipped over by a giant's finger, people stumbled and scrambled. A fat man on the step above the two girls stepped backward onto Sally's foot.

"Ow!" she yelped. He muttered an apology.

By that time they had nearly reached the top. A thin girl was

1

kneeling beside the top step, yanking at a wad of papers that was being ground to shreds between the steel lip and the moving steps. People were tripping over her as they left the escalator. Books and notebooks were strewn for yards around, getting kicked and trampled.

Sally glanced back, saw people still crowding on at the bottom, and yelled downward. "Hit the emergency button! Somebody's caught!" A moment later the steps slid to a halt. There was a lot of complaining as the escalator slowly emptied downward.

Tasha started picking up scattered books while Sally knelt beside the girl. "You're Valerie Hewens, aren't you? I'm Sally Sharp. I've seen you around at school."

She looked down at the papers wedged into the jaws of the escalator. Half of a neatly typed title showed. Valerie's effort to free it had given her only a handful of ripped pieces.

Valerie pushed strands of dark hair back from tear-streaked cheeks. "That was my English literature essay, due Monday. I guess now it's toast."

Tasha set a stack of books on the floor beside her. "Can't you reprint it?"

Valerie shook her head. "That's my only copy. I accidentally deleted the file from my laptop, which was smart! I worked on it a week, too."

"We'll get the janitor to reverse the escalator," Sally said.

"They can do that?" Valerie managed a shaky smile. "If I can get this mess out of here, at least I can retype it." She touched Sally's hand and added, "Thanks. I'm okay now."

A chorus of whoops and applause broke out behind them. Valerie looked back over her shoulder. "That bunch again! Those are the ones who knocked me down." Five or six kids were kicking a battered textbook back and forth across the marble floor, shrieking with laughter whenever another section of pages flew out.

Sally jumped to her feet. "Stop that!" They laughed and kept it up.

Tasha scowled. "That's it. I have *had* it!" She strode forward, her dark eyes flaring. Using her sturdy body like a battering ram, she decked the nearest boy off his feet. He landed in a flailing heap. Then she scooped up the book and stepped back.

The laughter died. Sally quickly stepped up beside Tasha. She was aware of Valerie at her other elbow. The book-molesters spread out in a line facing them. The boy Tasha had decked climbed to his feet, rubbing his elbow and looking furious.

They were all dressed in variations of the same outfit: ripped designer jeans, expensive leather jackets in spite of the hot weather, and heavy construction boots with the laces undone and flopping. And menacing expressions.

Sally thought she recognized some of the faces, but she was too busy trying to figure a way out of this situation to start remembering names. Where were the mall cops when you needed them?

"Guess who? Sally Snoop," cooed a tall, pencil-thin girl with a cap of ice-blond hair.

"Hi, Alys." Sally recalled her now. Alys Krug had just finished Grade 12, a year ahead of her at Knollvale High, so she knew her only by reputation. And that reputation wasn't good.

Alys tilted her head at Tasha. "That's a rough customer you run with, Sally."

"You started it," Tasha snapped.

"Right. Next time you're feeling playful, find a football field." Sally smiled, radiating a confidence she didn't feel. If this crew decided to get mean, the three of them didn't stand much of a chance.

Then her smile brightened. Three husky security guards were pushing through the crowd toward them. The ice princess spotted them at almost the same moment, shrugged, turned and strutted away. Her friends followed her.

"Rough, tough cream puffs!" Tasha laughed.

Valerie looked after them and shook her head. "I wouldn't trust them to back off next time."

"Right," Sally said. "We'd better keep an eye out for trouble after this."

Valerie knelt and started gathering up her books and as many papers as she could salvage, and stuffing them into her bag. She looked up as Sally and Tasha got down beside her. "You guys, I'm sorry you got mixed up in this."

"Never mind." Sally smiled. "You couldn't expect us to just look the other way, could you? Now, let's go find the janitor."

Chapter 2

Fabulous News

"SAL! TASH! Over here!" A small silhouette was bobbing up and down in front of a sunlit window, waving both hands in the air. Fay dropped back into her seat as the three other girls squeezed sideways between the crowded tables. Jo-Jo's was packed right out the doors.

"I've been defending this table with my life! Where've you been?" The bright light streaming through the window picked out indigo gleams in Fay's long, glossy black hair. "Hey there." She nodded at Valerie. "Somebody's going to have to sit on the window sill. I could only hold onto three chairs."

"I'll take the sill." Valerie dropped her heavy bag onto the floor. "Thanks for including me," she added softly.

Sally gave her a smile. "You looked like you could use some cheering up, even after you got your mangled essay back. Have you had a lot of trouble with those idiots?"

"Oh... not really." She didn't seem to want to talk about it, so after they'd ordered spicy fries and soft drinks, Sally gave Fay the gist of what happened on the escalator. As soon as Fay heard the name Hewens, she sat up straight and stared wide-eyed at Valerie.

"Wait just a second! Are you related to Peter Hewens? Please, please say yes!"

"Well, yes. He's my brother."

"Oh, fantastic! Let me show you what I bought for the audition, I need your opinion." She grabbed a shopping bag from under her chair and fished out a long, crocheted turquoise tunic. "I got matching

5

tights, too. What d'you think?" She looked expectantly from face to face. Then saw their puzzled expressions, and burst out laughing.

Sally Sharp, Tasha Dolinski and Fay Chen. The three of them were solid friends, and had been since preschool — hard though that was for most people to understand. Each was very different from the others in looks, personality, and interests. You wouldn't expect them to have a single thing in common. And yet they harmonized "like apple pie, ice cream and cheddar cheese," as Sally once said.

Tasha grinned affectionately at Fay. "Start at the beginning, okay, kid? And take it slow."

Fay sat back and mimed astonishment. "Don't tell me you never heard of Peter Hewens!" Their orders of spicy fries arrived, but she hardly noticed. "Peter Hewens, of Jones & Hewens? You were both with me when we saw him on TV last week. Come on!"

"Oh, now I remember." Sally's eyebrows went up. No wonder Fay was up in the air!

Jones & Hewens was a new and growing fashion design house based just outside Knollvale. At twenty-two Peter was very young to be a head designer, but you soon saw why he was such a success. His clothes were stunning, yet fun and relaxed. And it didn't hurt at all that he was outstandingly handsome in a dark and brooding style.

Sally remembered there was some other news about Jones & Hewens too, something not so pleasant, but she'd forgotten the details. "That was a great video, Val."

"It must be amazing to have Peter Hewens for a brother!" Fay was breathless. "Imagine the clothes! You do get free samples, right?"

"Um... not really," Valerie said apologetically.

"Don't take Fay too seriously," Tasha said. "She's gaga over clothes. Not just interested, like normal people."

6

A smile warmed Valerie's pale face. "I can guess what you'll be doing tomorrow, Fay. Trying out for a job as a model, right?"

"You bet! That was my news, by the way." She scarfed down a stick of fried potato. "The ad was in the *Morning Record*. They want girls in their mid- to late teens to model their new line of fashions. You'll try out too, guys, won't you? I don't want to go by myself."

"I don't know." Sally nibbled a fry. "I don't think I have the right look. Not cute and perky enough."

Fay peered over the table at Sally's slim denim-clad five-foot-seven and sighed despairingly. "Well, if you don't have the right look, what chance have I got?" She wilted in her chair.

"It lets me out too." Tasha wiped a dab of barbecue sauce off her chin, but ignored the blob decorating the front of her white T-shirt. "Can you see me mincing around on a runway in spike heels, showing off fancy clothes?"

Valerie laughed. "I think you'd all be great. I know, because I used to model for Jones & Hewens myself. Maybe you're a few inches too short, Fay, but you've got the look. You know: young, bright, full of energy. There's a good reason why Ermine likes to use local teens instead of professional models."

"You really think I've got the look?" Fay perked up again.

"Absolutely. And that all-one-colour outfit is a good idea, it'll make you look taller. I'll warn you, though, the pay is the pits."

"Who cares? For the chance to wear those flash new outfits — and work close to Peter Hewens — I'd pay *him*! At least, I would if I could afford to."

"Who's Ermine, by the way?" Tasha asked.

"Ermine Jones, the other partner in the company. She... well, she's quite a lady." Valerie smiled again, but Sally thought she looked uncomfortable.

7

"You said you used to model for Jones & Hewens." Tasha looked around the crowded room, then lowered her voice, although she didn't need to. The noise level was as good as a privacy screen. "I remember hearing that a lot of girls quit when Mrs. Mahon was killed. No big surprise. I guess they freaked, or their parents did."

"Not me," Val said quickly. "I did stop modelling then, but not because of — of what happened that night. I just don't have the time any more. I've been doing remedial English and math this summer."

"Aha." Tasha nodded. "That explains the textbooks."

"I hope the bad publicity didn't hurt the firm too much," Sally said. Now that her memory was jogged, the details of the case came flying back.

It had happened three weeks ago. Jones & Hewens had been staging a fashion party in the home of Mrs. Janine Lightstone. Two important fashion editors from Toronto were there, and later the show was given rave reviews in the media.

Only one shadow fell across Jones & Hewens's triumph that evening, but it was a dark one. One of the guests, a Mrs. Kendra Mahon, had been found with her head bashed in.

"It was a terrible thing to happen," Val said. "But it had nothing to do with the show. The police found out there'd been a break-in, and Mrs. Mahon must have surprised the burglar." She forced a smile. "But you're right, it isn't good to have people think of a... a death every time they think of Jones & Hewens. That's why Peter and Ermine are so anxious to get on with business as usual."

Her hands tightened around her bottle of pop as she talked, and her eyes kept darting nervously over Sally's shoulder. Sally looked around and spotted Alys Krug sitting three or four tables away with a tall, muscular boy she hadn't seen before. His light brown hair was cut so short, he looked almost bald. As Sally watched, they both turned their heads and stared at her, their expressions hostile.

"Who's that guy with Alys?" Sally tilted her head in that direction.

"That's her boyfriend, Dylan Thatcher." Valerie shifted in her seat so she was facing away from the pair. "He goes to a private school."

Tasha stood up. "Well, I don't know about you three, but this place just got too crowded for me."

"Me too." Sally pushed back her chair, but stopped when Valerie put a hand on her arm.

"Sally, wait. Could I talk to you? In private, I mean. It'll only be a minute."

Sally looked a question at Tasha and Fay. Tasha shrugged. "Sure."

Fay picked up her shopping bags. "No problem! Sal, can I grab a lift? Great — see you in the parking lot." They threaded their way to the door.

Sally settled back into her chair. "Okay, Val," she said gently. "I can tell there's something wrong. Does it have to do with Alys and her pals?"

She glanced in that direction. Alys and Dylan were still staring openly. Valerie turned her face to the window and lowered her voice to a whisper. "It's more complicated than that. I — I can't talk here. Could you come to my place?"

"All right, if you'd feel more comfortable there. I could make it this evening some time."

"That would be terrific!" She pulled a piece of paper from her bag and wrote an address on it. "Sally, you don't know what this means to me. There's nobody else I can talk to. I really need help!"

Chapter 3

Vanished

IT WAS GROWING DARK that evening as Sally's apple-red Honda Civic turned the corner of the street where Valerie lived. Halfway down the block, a cluster of vehicles was parked in front of a duplex. Their revolving lights shot colour up and down the street.

Sally pulled in behind an ambulance and two police cruisers. She peered anxiously up at the house. It was number sixty, Valerie's address. What was going on?

As Sally climbed out of her car, two paramedics shuffled down the front steps of the duplex, carrying a stretcher between them. The figure on the stretcher lay still, its head heavily bandaged. Sally's breath caught with anxiety.

Then she saw that the hair straggling from under the bandage was white, not dark brown. But that didn't ease her mind much. Something bad happened here, and Valerie was too close to it.

Sally took a moment to check the surroundings of the house. It stood back from the sidewalk, screened by a thick hedge of closely planted lilacs along both sides and a row of Lombardy poplars across the front. None of the neighbours had come out, except for a woman who stood on a lawn across the street. She was tightly gripping the hands of two small children who were straining to get closer to the action.

The ambulance was heading away down the street as Sally ran up the front steps. She plowed straight into a uniformed policeman who was on his way out.

"Whoa there!" He grinned and held her off with both hands. "Who you looking for?"

"I'm a friend of Valerie Hewens. She lives upstairs. Is she all right?"

"You're her friend?" His grin faded. "I think you better come in."

A chunky man in a suit and tie strode out into the lobby as Sally crossed the threshold. "Okay, Zack, I heard. Get on with it." He sounded irritated. His small mud-brown eyes snapped with impatience. "Who are you and what are you doing here?"

Reminding herself that this grump was a hard-working policeman trying to do his job, she took a deep breath and answered as nicely-yet-confidently as she knew how. "I'm Sally Sharp. Valerie asked me to come over this evening. Where is she?"

"My guess is, she's on the road to the airport by now." He stared at her face, alert for her reaction.

"Airport? Why there?"

"You tell me."

Sally felt baffled and annoyed. "You haven't identified yourself," she pointed out coolly.

"Detective R.J. Braun, KPD Homicide."

"Homicide?" Her heart flipped. "But—"

Running feet pounded up the front steps. The man who burst into the lobby seemed to fill it. Not that he was especially large, but he radiated nervous energy. He skidded to a halt a stride away from the detective and flung a mane of black hair back from a face that was pale with strain. His eyes were dark with emotion.

"What's happened here? Where's my sister?"

"Calm down, Mr. Hewens. Far's I know, she's okay. The old lady she bashed over the head isn't doing so good, though."

Peter Hewens froze. In the next second or two Sally had a chance

11

to really look at him. On TV, his good looks had been obvious. But the camera hadn't captured his vitality. She found it hard to take her eyes off him.

He was wearing a grey tweed jacket over a shirt of muted blue plaid and slim jeans. Somehow the outfit managed to look both relaxed and fashionable, although it was less funky than she would have expected to see on a rising young designer.

After a long stare he unfroze. "Is this some sick joke?"

Detective Braun turned away into the ground floor apartment. "C'mon in and see. Don't touch anything."

Once inside, Sally scanned the room and shaped a silent whistle. It was a mess. A small desk had been rifled, every drawer dumped on the carpet. Books lay scattered across the floor, and a row of collector plates on a sideboard had been smashed.

Peter gasped. "There's been a break-in! Where's Val?"

"Where indeed," Braun said dryly.

"Mrs. Engstrom. You said she was hurt." Peter clenched his fists. "Val never did that!"

"And a lot of this," Sally pointed around the room, "is just plain mindless vandalism. Val wouldn't do that either. She isn't like that."

"You'll forgive me if I don't call off the search on your say-so, Miss Sharp." Braun's thick eyebrows pulled together. "That name rings a bell." He stared at her. Then his frown deepened. "Oh, yeah. I've heard about you. And your mother." His tone said he wasn't impressed.

Sally startled to bristle up, then took a breath and told herself it wasn't worth getting steamed up about. In the past year she'd come in contact with the Knollvale police a few times, starting from when she'd helped her school principal clear up some problems. First there'd been that series of thefts from lockers, and later a nasty case of anonymous bullying.

After that, people — kids at school and some adults in her neighbourhood — began to think of her as a crime-solver. Among other things, she was asked to find a lost laptop, catch someone who was stealing Christmas parcels from mailboxes, trap an intruder in an attic (it turned out to be a raccoon) and identify a gang of teens who were breaking car windows and stealing electronics.

Some of these cases brought Sally and her friends Tasha and Fay into contact with the police. She was used to getting a mixed reaction. A few members of the force had become allies and even friends. Others were skeptical or hostile, thinking she was just a kid playing detective — like, they assumed, her mystery-writing mother. It was clear which camp this man belonged to, but she wasn't going to let him get her down.

"What makes you so sure Val did this?" she asked. "Did Mrs. Engstrom see her?"

"We can't be sure about that yet," he said grudgingly, "but it's obvious. Mrs. Engstrom heard somebody in her kitchen and she guessed it would be Valerie. Seems she — the girl — is in the habit of walking in at all hours."

"Why not?" Peter stepped forward angrily. "They're old friends. And Mrs. Engstrom leaves her door unlocked all the time."

"Yeah, yeah, I know." Braun raised a calming hand. "Only, this time it looks like your sister had more in mind than a social call. Because when the old lady walked into the kitchen, somebody walloped her on the head from behind." He paused to let this sink in, while he scanned their faces. Peter just shook his head furiously.

"So she never saw who attacked her," Sally said.

"She may have. Looks like she half-turned, so the blow landed on the side of her head instead of the back. Then she was able to get to the phone and call 911 before she collapsed. All the money was gone from her purse. Not that she had much," he added in a tone of contempt for the thief. Sally had to agree with him there.

"Look." Peter pulled himself together. "Just because Val isn't here doesn't mean she did this. I'm telling you, she couldn't have! Mrs. Engstrom was like a grandmother to her."

Braun cocked his head. "So where is she?"

"How should I know? Out with a friend — shopping — she could be anywhere!"

"Uh-uh. Miss Sharp, here, says she was supposed to meet your sister here this evening. What about?" His eyes narrowed on her.

"I don't know for sure. She just said she wanted to talk." Sally had an idea what it was about, but she wasn't ready to share that yet.

"Okay, you two. C'mon upstairs."

Chapter 4

Suspicion of Murder

AS THEY STARTED up the stairs leading to the second floor, Peter stood aside and swept out a hand. "After you, Sally." It was the first sign that he'd noticed she was there. He even attempted a smile, although it wasn't much of a success.

Nothing seemed out of place in the Hewens apartment. Sally noted the luxurious carpet and soft leather sofa, and her eyebrows rose. "Tell me if I'm wrong, but I don't think Val would've had to rob an old woman to get travelling money."

"Depends how far she wanted to travel, doesn't it?" Braun grunted. He strode along a short corridor leading to the rear of the apartment. They followed him into the first of two rooms.

It looked as if a tornado had swept through it and blown away about half the contents. Dresser drawers hung out, empty. The closet door was open, showing a rack of hangers and nothing else.

"As you can see," Braun said, "she took almost everything but her school work. Guess she doesn't plan to do much studying, wherever she's going."

Books lay open on the blue satin bedspread, as well as a scatter of torn paper and a laptop computer. Sally took a closer look. The laptop was in screensaver mode. Careful not to touch anything with her hands, she joggled the bed slightly with one knee. The screensaver vanished and a document displayed. She shook her head. "This doesn't make a lot of sense."

"You're telling me!" Peter burst out.

15

"Val was only halfway through copying out this essay. Look, she stopped in the middle of a word." Sally pointed. "Why would she carefully do half her assignment, then break off — right in the middle of a word — to go downstairs and bash someone?"

"That's what we'll have to find out, isn't it?" Braun looked at Peter. "Where would she keep her suitcase? What's it look like?"

"In the basement. All our luggage is in a row at the back. Hers is a set in cream-coloured leather."

"Just a minute." Braun went out, and they heard him shouting directions from the top of the stairs. Peter's wide eyes met Sally's. He looked as if he was still in shock.

"If it's any help," she said, "I'm as stunned as you are. I don't know your sister really well, but she made an impression on me today. And none of this," she waved a hand around, "fits that impression."

He shot her a grateful look, and his mouth relaxed. It gave her a hint of how handsome he would look when he wasn't worried out of his mind.

But there was no time to talk before Detective Braun came back. "There's two cream-coloured pieces there, a big garment bag and a little tote thing. And a gap between them. What's missing?"

Peter's mouth twisted. "Val's weekender."

Sally's heart sank. This could be bad.

Braun was looking at Peter with what could have been a glint of pity in his hard eyes. "I'm going to let you in on something. I figure you won't blab it around, and it'll make some sense of this for you. And, Miss Sharp..." His eyes flicked at her. "Once you know the facts, you'll see there's no mystery here. Just one scared, mixed-up little girl."

Peter shoved his fists in his pockets. "Well?"

16

"You're aware I've been checking on some thefts that might be connected to your company, Mr. Hewens."

Peter nodded, but Sally frowned. "What thefts?"

"Oh, minor stuff. Small bits of jewellery, figurines, watches, missing from houses." The detective scratched the bald spot on the crown of his head. "But it's suggestive that each of those thefts was discovered soon after Jones & Hewens gave a fashion party at the house in question."

Sally's eyes widened. "You think one of the models was stealing? One of the girls?"

"Who else? Not too likely either Mr. Hewens or Miss Jones would want to risk damaging the good name of their company, just so's they could pick up a trinket here or there. But it's exactly the kind of mindless thing some kids would do."

Sally opened her mouth to protest, then decided to save her breath. This man wasn't one you could reason with.

"It's not the kind of thing Valerie does," Peter said fiercely. "She's not like that at all. What makes you pick on her?"

"She's run off, hasn't she? None of the other girls has skipped town."

"Some proof!"

"I'll get proof, don't you worry." Braun turned away with a shrug. "Soon's we find her."

"You still haven't explained why she would panic and run off in the middle of doing her homework," Sally said. "Or why she would hurt Mrs. Engstrom."

"No problem there." Braun strolled around the room, his eyes probing into the corners. "The way I see it, she's no hardened criminal. Suppose she went into the old lady's place, not meaning any harm, then saw her purse and just couldn't resist."

Peter flared up again. "Val's not a kleptomaniac!"

"I didn't say that. Let me talk. She hears the old lady coming, knows she'll be caught with her hand in the till, so to speak, panics and lashes out. Pure reflex. Then she can't face what she's done, and she runs. It's an old story."

Peter sank onto Valerie's blue satin bedspread and buried his face in his hands. Sally bit her lip. Thinking back, she recalled Val's nervousness that afternoon. Sign of a troubled conscience? What had she wanted to talk about that she couldn't tell anybody else? Was it the thefts Braun had described?

There was just a chance Detective Braun might be on the right track. But Peter looked so desperate, Sally couldn't say so.

She crossed the room to where Braun was standing at the window. "No wonder the neighbours didn't come out." She pushed the drapes aside. "With all those bushes, they probably didn't see a thing. But have you talked to the woman across the street?"

"One of my men is doing that now. Got any more tips for me, Detective Inspector Sharp?" He grinned sarcastically.

"Just one." She met his eyes. "I'm almost certain Valerie wanted my help because she was being harassed by a group of teens. Two of them were watching us today. Alys Krug and Dylan Thatcher. You might check out where they were this evening."

"You trying to teach me my job?" Before she could answer, he turned and pushed past her. The blue drapes swung back against the wall with a dull clunk. Braun stopped. "What's this?"

Sally knelt swiftly and turned the bottom of the drape so they could see the back. Three or four inches of stitching had been pulled out of the deep hem, creating a pocket. "Something's in here. Something heavy." She started to reach inside, but Braun stopped her with a touch on the wrist.

"What is it?" Peter got up off the bed.

"Dunno... yet." Braun pulled a packet from inside his coat, drew out a pair of thin white latex gloves, and put them on. Then he dipped into the hem pocket and brought out a polished silver statue about the size of his palm: a girl in a flowing dress and big hat, holding a staff with a crook on the end.

"Looks like Little Bo-Peep: the one who lost her sheep," Sally said. Glancing at Braun's grim expression, she had a feeling this was not something to joke about.

"It is. It's one of a set of a dozen silver figurines, all about characters from nursery rhymes."

Peter cleared his throat. "How do you know?"

"Because it was stolen from the Lightstone house, the night Mrs. Mahon was murdered. In fact, it was taken from the room where her body was found." Braun rose to his feet. "And now it shows up here. I guess your sister's not just a thief, Mr. Hewens. Could be I'm looking for a killer."

Chapter 5
Sally on the Case

PETER STOOD AT THE bay window of his living room, scowling down at the street below. The two police cars were pulling away from the curb.

He slammed his fist against the wall. "Can you believe that guy? My sister a murderer! If he hadn't been a cop I would've..." He clenched his fist, then dropped it in frustration and thumped down on the leather sofa beside Sally.

"Now we know why a homicide detective has been dealing with the thefts," she said thoughtfully. "Braun has been checking out anything even remotely connected to the Mahon murder. Finding that figurine in Valerie's room is a real break for him because it wraps up all the crimes into one neat package."

"But—"

"Take it easy!" She put a hand on his sleeve. "I don't think Val's a killer any more than you do. And I don't think she attacked Mrs. Engstrom. That scenario of Braun's doesn't hang together."

"Scenario?" Peter rubbed tired-looking eyes.

"Remember his guess that Val hit out in panic because she was caught red-handed?"

"Yeah. He said it probably happened that way when Mrs. Mahon was killed, too." He grimaced.

"The problem with that is, Mrs. Engstrom was hit from *behind* by someone who was waiting behind a door. That sounds pretty cool and calculated to me."

20

Peter sat up straighter. "That's right! Why didn't you say so to Braun?"

"Because he wouldn't have wanted to hear it from me." She made a face. "His mind's made up. It'll take more than your faith in Val, or my opinion, to change it. It'll take hard facts. And we don't have any of those."

Peter jumped up off the sofa, paced back and forth, then whirled around and stared down at her. "I don't care what kind of mess Val's in, I just know she hasn't done anything bad."

"I believe that too."

"Then help me prove it! You're her friend, right?"

She looked up at him, troubled. "Yes, but—"

"And you've solved criminal cases before, so I've heard. So—"

"I've solved crimes, yes, but not like this! Nothing involving murder!"

He waved his hands. "You wouldn't have to deal with the murder. I agree, leave that to the police. You'd only have to find out what's happened to Val. Once she's found, I'm certain she'll clear everything up."

She hesitated. "I couldn't promise anything."

"I wouldn't expect miracles." He sat down beside her again and took her hand in both of his. "But, Sally, I've heard about you. I've heard about the people you've helped. The police have made up their minds Val's guilty, so — who else can I turn to?"

His eyes were dark and sad until he smiled at her, and then they were warm and soft. Sally couldn't help smiling back at him.

"All right, I'll try."

He laughed, dropped her hands and caught her in a quick hug. She was breathless when he let her go.

She caught her breath. "Okay! Let's get started. Have you no-

21

ticed Val seeming troubled lately? Was there any phone call that seemed to upset her, for example, or a problem at school? Did she mention any names?"

Peter looked guilty. "To be honest, we haven't talked much lately. I've been run off my feet getting our next collection ready for the September shows."

"Could she have confided in anyone else?" But Sally already knew the answer. Valerie had come to her for advice because she had nobody else to confide in.

"The only person I can think of is Mrs. Engstrom. She became a sort of grandmother figure to Val after we moved here, since our parents and our grandparents are all dead."

"Then there's a place to start." Sally sprang to her feet and headed for the door. "Oh, and don't be surprised if you see me at Jones & Hewens tomorrow, trying out for a modelling job."

"You want a job?" His eyebrows rose.

"I'm not asking you to get me hired." She laughed. "I just want a chance to nose around a bit."

"But you said you didn't think Val had anything to do with those thefts."

"I didn't say that," she answered carefully. That question was still open in her own mind. "I said she had nothing to do with the killing. But there's that figurine we found in her room..."

"An obvious frame-up!"

"It could be. If it is, the real thief may also be connected to Jones & Hewens. I think Braun's on the right track, he just stopped following it too soon."

SALLY'S MIND was busy as the red Honda sped across town toward Knollvale Hospital. If luck was with her, the old lady would be

22

conscious and able to see visitors. And perhaps able to reveal what had been preying on Valerie's mind. Better yet, she might be able to identify her attacker.

But when Sally stopped at the admissions desk and asked for directions, the answer was ominous. The technician turned cheerfully to her computer screen and scrolled down a few lines, then her smile faded. "I'm sorry, you won't be able to see her."

Sally's mouth felt dry. This could only mean one thing. "You mean she's... died?"

"Oh! No. But she's in a coma. The doctors say she may or may not recover." The woman looked at her sympathetically. "I'm sorry. Are you a relative?"

"No, just a friend of a friend."

Sally shivered as she walked out into the dark parking lot. *Coma... may or may not recover...* It must have taken a vicious blow to cause damage that severe. Valerie was mixed up in something bad.

Another thought crossed Sally's mind. Despite the signs that Val ran away, there was no real proof that she'd gone willingly.

Or even that she was still alive.

Chapter 6

Walking the Walk

"OH, SALLY, WHY did I ever think I had a chance?" Fay curled her crochet-clad legs under her chair.

"I think you've got a really good chance," Sally whispered back. "You're cuter than any of these girls, and you move better than most."

"Right, watch that one!" Tasha nodded at a tall brunette who was teetering along on high heels. "All the grace of a three-legged giraffe."

"Better a giraffe than a hamster!"

Sally stifled a laugh. "I'll bet Ms. Jones doesn't think so." Ermine Jones was a slim woman in her thirties with short, fashionably styled auburn hair. Her outfit — perfectly fitted jeans and an indigo velvet jacket — was understated, yet somehow had more impact than any of the gaudy clothes the girls were wearing. Right now she was watching the brunette with a look of tightly reined impatience.

The Jones & Hewens showroom took up a quarter of the ground floor of a renovated farmhouse outside town. This was where they displayed their new clothing lines to buyers from the stores. This Sunday afternoon, the rows of folding chairs were filled with — Sally counted — at least seventy teenaged girls. The place buzzed with giggles and whispers. A few of the girls were treating the audition as a game, but most of them were simmering with serious excitement.

Since Sally didn't expect to be hired, she was cool and relaxed. Or thought she was. She knew she was looking her best today. She had chosen a sapphire silk-knit dress that flattered her slim figure and echoed the blue of her eyes.

"Thanks, Lisa. Sit down, please." Ms. Jones penciled a word or two on her clipboard. Then raised her head. "Sally Sharp!"

Startled, Sally jumped from her chair and walked forward, aware of Fay and Tasha hissing encouragement from behind. She swept a look around the roomful of critical eyes and felt her whole body stiffen up. Her smooth walk became a jerky stride.

"Just relax, Sally," came a friendly voice. She turned to meet the warm brown eyes of Ermine Jones.

Sally smiled back at her. It was like being on stage in the school play, she told herself. She'd done scarier things before this. She took a deep breath. Her fluttering heartbeat calmed down. She moved confidently across the floor, turned around once, and walked back.

"Thank you, Sally." This time Ermine penciled in a few words before calling the next name. As Sally plopped back into her chair, Fay grabbed her hand.

"You're in, I just know it!"

Tasha groaned. "I've decided I don't want to do this. I'm dressed all wrong and I feel ridiculous!"

Sally elbowed her in the ribs. "You're not backing out now!"

"There, she's calling your name," Fay whispered. "Go!" She gave Tasha a push.

"Oh, all right!" Tasha shot out of her chair and strode across the floor. Halfway across she stubbed her toe and fell onto one knee. From yards away Sally could hear her cotton skirt ripping, and her heart dropped into her shoes in sympathy.

Tasha bounced up again in a flash, grinned around at the ring of smirking faces, and finished her walk with a cheerful wave. "I know, I blew it," she muttered as she sat down. "What do I care? It's over!"

She settled back comfortably to watch.

Fifteen minutes later Fay's name was called. She took a deep, shaky breath. "Wish me luck!" Sally crossed her fingers and Tasha did the same.

Despite her nervousness, once Fay started moving she was all confidence. Instead of just walking she danced lightly across the floor, eyes bright. At the turn she spun gracefully, her long black hair spraying out around her shoulders, then came sailing back. She looked radiant.

"Ladies and gents, we have a winner!" Sally murmured. Tasha clapped softly. And Ermine Jones was smiling.

Chapter 7

Welcome to Jones & Hewens

"DON'T LOOK SO guilty, you two." Fay forced a smile. "I'm glad you got in, Sal. Now you'll be able to sleuth without being too obvious about it."

During the drive to the farmhouse, Sally had given Fay and Tasha the gist of what happened last night. Fay was right: her being hired could be a lucky break. "All the same, I wish you'd made it too."

Tasha gave Fay a hug. "If it weren't so awful for you, it'd be funny. I still can't fathom why she hired me, after the klutz I made of myself."

"I can," Fay said brightly. "Miss Jones liked the way you bounced back. And you'll look terrific in their sportswear. I wish... well, never mind."

"You can kick me if it'll make you feel better." Tasha stuck out an ankle and gritted her teeth.

Fay laughed. "Don't tempt me!" She glanced at the open door, where the last of the also-rans were filing out. "I'll go wait in your car, Sally. No point in my hanging around in here."

"Fay, wait!" Ermine Jones strode along the hall, waving her clipboard. "I'm glad I caught you. I could tell how disappointed you were not to be hired. But, to be honest..."

"I know. It's because I'm a shrimp. It's okay, Miss Jones."

"Not a shrimp!" Ermine laughed. "Petite, I'd have said. In every other way, you're perfect for Jones & Hewens. You're really hooked on the fashion industry, aren't you? How'd you like to work here as an assistant?"

Fay's eyes widened. Her mouth opened, but no sound came out. Tasha poked her in the side and she squeaked, "Oh, wow! You mean, actually work with you and... and Peter?" She breathed his name reverently.

Ermine's brown eyes twinkled. "It wouldn't be a bit glamorous. You'd be doing everything from filing and answering phones to helping the models dress to sweeping up fabric scraps. Still hooked?"

"When can I start?" Fay was all but levitating.

"Why not right now? Come on, girls, I'll grab the others and we'll take the grand tour." She strode off, beckoning over her shoulder with the clipboard.

IN ALL, SIX GIRLS had been hired. Besides Sally and Tasha, the lucky ones were Misty LeBrun, a red-haired girl who moved like a dancer, and Dena Mendez, a slim girl with a long fall of soft dark hair.

"Miss Jones? That's only four," Fay noted.

"Two of last season's girls are still with us. And by the way, you can drop the Miss Jones. Call me Ermine, okay?" She gave them a wry grin. "How my parents came up with Ermintrude I'll never know, but — as you can guess — I shortened it the first chance I got!"

Laughter rippled through the knot of girls as they followed her through a door at the end of the showroom. "Isn't she great?" Fay whispered. Sally nodded, but she was too busy looking around to answer.

"This is our work area." Ermine swept out an arm. The room was huge. Its utilitarian look was softened by the light pouring in through

28

big windows. A wall of mirrors doubled the light. Over the buzz of sewing machines rose a hum of cheerful voices.

At the far end, three grey-haired women sat at machines, sewing, in front of a wall rack that held hundreds of spools of thread in every colour you could imagine. Bolts of cloth were stacked on shelves and stood on end in corners. The centre of the room was dominated by a long table where two younger women were arranging pattern pieces on a length of fabric.

"As you can see, this is a hands-on operation," Ermine said. "There are machines that automatically cut out the pieces, guided by a pattern in the computer, but we don't do that here."

Fay nudged Sally. "Do you see who I see? Doesn't he look fabulous?"

Peter was kneeling beside a motionless mannequin, frowning as he altered the fit of a cream-coloured dress. Sally had to admit that "fabulous" was a fair description. Appreciative murmurs floated among the girls. He didn't seem to hear them.

But the mannequin did. It gave Sally a jolt when the figure she'd thought was a lifeless dummy turned its blond head and looked back over its shoulder. A glimpse of ice-pale eyes gave her another jolt.

Tasha drew in a quick breath. "Alys Krug!"

Chapter 8

Behind the Glamour

"PETER AND I each have an office." Ermine nodded at two doors opening off the main room. "But Peter likes to work on his designs out here."

The corner table she pointed at was littered with markers and coloured pencils. Half a dozen sketches were pinned to the wood-plank wall nearby. Dena Mendez gazed at them with awe. "Where does he get his ideas?"

Ermine held up her hands. "Beats me! He's the creative genius around here, I'm just the organizer. But perhaps he'll tell you."

At this Peter rose from his knees and gave Ermine a strained smile. He looked as if he hadn't slept much last night, and wouldn't appreciate having to discuss his ideas with a flock of adoring girls.

Sally didn't blame him one bit. She already knew, having asked Detective Braun by telephone, that Valerie was still missing, and there was no evidence of her having boarded any airplane, train, or bus.

"On this long table," Ermine continued, "we draft the paper pattern from his design, then the first garment is made up in white muslin. It's called a toile. Then it's fitted to a live model."

Fay studied Alys critically. "Why that sort of no-colour cloth? It looks so... well..."

"Boring?" Ermine smiled. "True, but it gives us a chance to correct our fitting mistakes before we cut the good fabric. That's what Peter's doing right now: fitting the toile. How's it coming, Peter?"

"Uh... coming along just fine, Ermine." He smiled at the girls, but the good cheer looked forced. Abruptly, he turned and headed into his office. The door closed behind him. Sally saw a shadow pass over Ermine's face.

Then she brightened again and laid a hand on Alys's shoulder. "Alys Krug is our fitting model because she's a perfect size six: right in the middle of our size range. Alys and her sister Natasha have been with us for a year, so if you have any questions about modelling, just ask them. I'm sure they'd both be glad to share what they know."

Alys tossed back her short, silky blond hair and gave them all a tight smile.

"Yeah, likely," muttered Tasha in the rear.

Ermine went on to describe how a master pattern was made from the toile, then how samples were made up in the chosen fabric.

"Always, of course, with our trademark corduroy rose somewhere in the design. Here's an example, girls. These are part of next spring's line." She beckoned them over to a rack where several outfits were hanging.

Fay reached out and fingered the material. "Oh, don't I wish!" The calf-length silken skirts were slit high in several places, so the wearer would be walking in a flurry of brilliant streamers. Long, straight jackets cut from a velvety pinwale corduroy contained the look, and on each collar was a rose made of the same material in a contrasting colour: garnet on emerald, mint green on plum, gold on indigo.

Dena looked puzzled. "Did you say these are for next spring? But it's only August! Why so early?"

"Because fashions go into the stores well before the season, and it takes time to create and produce a line of clothing. We start work at least six months ahead."

"And those three sewing ladies supply all the stores?" Dena was wide-eyed.

Ermine laughed. "No, a contractor in Cambridge does that — that's where you'd find the computer-guided cutting machines. Our ladies make the samples for our shows."

While she described the way Jones & Hewens's fashions were produced, Sally's mind was busy. She was sorting out the implications of Alys having worked at Jones & Hewens for a whole season, at the same time as Valerie. A sudden suspicion chilled her.

As if Alys had read her thoughts, the pale grey eyes locked sharply on hers. Then a smug, innocent mask slid down over Alys's face.

"Now, girls!" Ermine perched on the edge of the cutting table, looked around at the ring of expectant faces, and became crisp and businesslike. "Tonight's your trial by fire. Your first fashion show. Everybody up for it?"

Misty LeBrun clapped her hands to her mouth. "Tonight? Omigosh! What about our training? I mean, aren't you going to teach us how to walk like professionals?"

A chorus of agreement followed. Ermine shook her head. "If I'd wanted professionals I would've hired them. Alys and I will teach you how to display the outfits to their best advantage, but beyond that I want you to just be yourselves. Any other questions?"

"Where's tonight's show?" asked Tasha.

"At the home of Mrs. Edwina Creel. The occasion is a party for her oldest daughter, and a good thick layer of the social cream will be there. Also, I hope, a reporter from *Women's Wear Daily*. I expect to sell some of the outfits, but the real purpose is publicity for our new Corduroy Rose label. The right sort of publicity, of course."

Ermine's mouth tightened. Sally guessed she was thinking of the

32

Mahon murder. She cleared her throat. "Ermine, this may be a stupid question, but why not just hold one big show, like other fashion designers?"

"That's not a stupid question at all." Ermine nodded at her. "It's because Jones & Hewens isn't like the rest. We do things our way! Energy, verve and fun — that's what we're all about, and that's what you girls will be projecting tonight! So, tell me again — are you up for it?"

"Yes!" "You bet!" Sally found herself laughing and bouncing with the rest. Ermine's enthusiasm was infectious.

But not everybody was swept away, she noticed. Alys Krug wore a faintly mocking smile as she looked on.

Ermine beamed. "Terrific! Now, I'm going to discuss hair styles, then Alys will give you a crash course on runway modelling." She slipped off the table and started back to the showroom, trailed by the girls.

At the door she turned. "Not that I want to give anyone the jitters," she added mischievously, "but let me remind you that every move you make tonight will be captured on camera!"

Chapter 9

Gossip Girls

LATE AFTERNOON sunshine was raying out from between the clouds when the girls left the back door of the farmhouse and headed for their cars. As the door closed behind them, Tasha exploded with a whoop and did an angry jig on the gravel. The others burst out laughing.

"What a slave driver that Alys is!" Misty gasped. "And oh, Tasha, did she ever have it in for you!

"I swear," Tasha growled through gritted teeth, "if she'd made one more 'stumblebum' remark, I would've hauled off and let her have it on the schnozz!"

"Especially considering you sailed through the routine without a mistake the last time," Fay added.

Sally paused with her hand on the door of her car. Here was a chance to encourage gossip, and see what turned up. "Loved that silk jacket she had on, though. Isn't she a dynamite dresser?"

Dena Mendez tossed her long hair and shrugged. "I guess you have to give her that. But I don't know how she does it. It's not like her family's well off, and those clothes of hers aren't cheap."

"You mean, where she does she get things like that flashy gold watch?" Misty said. "It's got to be fake."

"No," Fay put in, "it's the real thing. I noticed it too. And I've got an eye for that kind of stuff." She pointed seriously at her peepers.

"It can't be real. She's such a phony!" Misty giggled. "Like the

34

way she spells her name. I'll bet it's A-l-i-c-e on her birth certificate! And she likes to make out she's part of that rich crowd the Thatchers belong to, but she totally isn't."

Sally wrinkled her forehead. "Thatcher?"

"Her boyfriend. Dylan Thatcher. His folks are loaded. Not that that makes him a cool kind of guy, not at all," Misty added with a grimace.

Tasha caught Sally's eye and nodded slightly. "Didn't I hear something about him a while back?"

"You mean the time he was caught breaking into the office at school?" Dena suggested.

"That's it. Wasn't he arrested?"

Misty laughed. "Are you kidding? He wasn't even suspended. His folks got him off, of course. That creep thinks he can get away with murder!" She headed toward her car, adding, "Dena? If you need a ride, come on."

The other three waved and chorused, "See you tonight!"

It seemed very quiet after Misty's car rounded the farmhouse and vanished up the lane leading through the woods to the highway. Wind sighed through the trees. The sunlight was fading again behind the clouds. Sally shivered, although the air was still warm.

"Getting the creeps, Sal?" Fay gazed around. "Me too. I don't know how Ermine can stand to live out here all on her own. There's a sad feeling to this place when the sun's not shining, isn't there?"

"Yeah." Tasha, who had her own car, a rusting ten-year-old Ford Taurus, pulled out her keys and tossed them in one hand. "Maybe that's because it used to be a working farm and it's gone back to brush. See that ruin over there in the woods? I'll bet it used to be the barn. The place feels abandoned, but there's no mystery about that."

"Still, it is a bit depressing," Sally said. "But that's not what gave me a chill. It's a train of thought that started when we spotted Alys in there. Remember how I thought Val wanted to talk to me because Alys and her gang were harassing her? I thought they were just being bullies."

Tasha stopped jingling her keys. "And then you found out about the thefts."

"You get what I'm thinking? Suppose Val knew or suspected something about the thefts? And suppose the bullying was a warning to keep her mouth shut?"

Fay blew out her cheeks. "That's a lot of supposes."

"Well, here's a couple of facts for you, then." Sally swung her car door open. "Alys saw Val and me with our heads together at Jo-Jo's, and a few hours later Val was gone. I can't help feeling there's a link."

"And knowing you," Tasha said dryly, "you feel responsible."

Sally grimaced unhappily. "Partly, yes. But there's more to it than that. The more I think about this case, the more I get the feeling that Alys and her boyfriend Dylan are right smack in the middle of it."

"Let's talk about it later." Fay slid into the passenger seat of the Honda. "You both should be home right now, doing your hair for to-night's show."

Doing her hair was the last thing on Sally's mind. As she sent the car purring along the highway toward Knollvale, a sentence was haunting her. *That creep thinks he can get away with murder!*

Chapter 10
Traces and Alibis

"BRAN, I'M HOME! Is Mom back yet?" Sally listened for a reply, but the house was silent. Then she caught sight of a yellow sticky note on the kitchen doorpost. The message, in her brother Brandon's looping scrawl, said: *Gone for pizza, back soon. Mom away 2 more days.*

Sally sighed. Their mother was spending two weeks teaching a short course in crime fiction writing at a college in Kingston. She'd been expected home today. It was a letdown that she wouldn't be.

Lacey Sharp was not just the author of a best-selling mystery series featuring the Mennonite detective Hannah Thiessen; she was also an expert on criminology — and an understanding mom. Lacey had never tried to tell her daughter how to handle any of her cases, no matter how harmless or how serious, but she was always available when Sally needed a sympathetic and interested listener.

Brandon, on the other hand, was no use at all when it came to talking over the murkier points of cases. At 19, two years older than Sally, he still treated her like his baby sister. And as a hard-headed engineering student at the University of Waterloo, he had no patience with her "playing detective." In that he was a lot like R.J. Braun, Sally reflected.

That thought reminded her of a call she had to make. Pulling out her cellphone, she punched in the Knollvale Police headquarters number and asked to be put through to Detective R.J. Braun. He took the call, which was a pleasant surprise, but he still sounded annoyed.

She wondered if this was his normal state of mind, or if she especially got on his nerves.

"I've heard Dylan Thatcher has been in trouble with the law," she said in her pleasantest tone. "Have you had a chance to check out his alibi?"

"As a matter of fact I'm way ahead of you, Miss Sharp. The night Kendra Mahon was killed, Dylan was in Mexico with his parents."

"Hm." She bit her lip. "That is some alibi. What about yesterday evening?"

Papers rustled at the other end. "He says he was out driving with some pals. The two other boys confirm that."

"Good friends of his?"

"If you mean would they lie to cover for him, yes, I suspect they would. That's not relevant."

Sally fought down an angry reply. "So your only suspect is Valerie Hewens? You're not following any other leads? What about Alys Krug?"

She heard him take a deep breath. When he spoke again she could tell he was holding his temper on a very short leash. "Alys Krug was home at the time of the attack on Mrs. Engstrom. Her mother confirms that. Now, Sally, you listen to me. One woman has died and another is in a coma, and Valerie Hewens is linked to both incidents. You just bet I'm going after her with all I've got!"

"And have you found any trace of her?"

"Not yet. Look, I'm very busy— "

"Just one more question. Who was it who found Mrs. Mahon's body? Was it Alys?"

Braun let out a bark of laughter. "No, it was your friend Peter Hewens. So why don't you leave me alone and pester him instead?" He hung up.

Sally stared at her phone. So Peter had found the body. Of course, that didn't mean much. But he should have mentioned it to her, especially if he wanted her to find Valerie. It struck her now that Peter had told her almost nothing about himself, or even about Valerie.

A moment after she slid her phone back in her pocket, it rang. "Sally? Peter here."

"Peter! I'm glad you called. I—"

"Please just listen." His voice was hard and clipped. "I've been to the hospital. Mrs. Engstrom isn't expected to recover. Were you aware of that? Sally, I've decided to accept the police line on this. I'm calling off your investigation."

Chapter 11

Enemy in Red

A CHANDELIER SPARKLED over Sally's head. She strode
smoothly across the polished terrazzo floor in time to the beat of re-
corded music.

Peter's amplified voice overrode the music for a moment. "Ladies, our Golden Girl!"

Smiling, Sally turned, then turned again, one hand on hip, to
show all sides of the short, flippy bronze silk dress, with its gold corduroy rose fastened on one shoulder. The other shoulder was bare. A
long gold silk scarf around her neck flew out behind when she
whirled to show how the dress moved. As she left the room, applause
broke out behind her.

She was still smiling as she hurried into the change room down
the hall. It was actually a washroom-powder room, but it was bigger
than most people's living rooms. The Creel house was a mansion, no
other word for it.

Right now the change room was chaotic with girls coming and
going, dressed and half-dressed. The air was electric. It was like
opening night before the curtain goes up on a new play, Sally
thought. She looked around for Tasha, then realized she must be out
on the floor now, showing a cruise outfit.

Since Sally was going to model only evening dresses at this
show, her next turn was at least twenty minutes away. But there was
no time to sit still. She pulled at her scarf, but the knot in back resisted her fingers. "Fay! Can you help me?"

"Just a sec, Sal!" Fay was struggling with a stuck zipper in the back of Natasha's dress.

Alys, who had been looking around at the excited group with a cool smile, pushed Fay aside. "Let me. I have a way with zippers."

"Thanks!" Fay ran to Sally and was getting to work on the knotted scarf when Misty called out.

"Oh, no! I'm next up and I've ripped my hem!"

Fay let out a muted scream. "I'm going crazy! Back in a minute, Sal." She hurried away, pulling a sewing kit from her pocket.

Sally looked across the room at Alys and Natasha. The sisters shared the same pale, sharp features and short, silky ash-blond hair. They would be going out as a pair. In identical crimson linen dresses and hats they might have been twins.

But there was no mistaking which was which if you really looked. Alys always wore a superior smile and carried herself like a pirate queen. Natasha, a year younger, was a timid girl who spoke softly and had trouble looking people in the eye. Sally wondered if a lifetime of having a pirate queen for an older sister could do that to you.

Ermine poked her head in the door. "Where's Misty? Not ready yet? Okay, let's have Alys and Natasha." They ran out hand in hand.

Tasha was back now, and Misty was next up. Sally looked at the clock. "Uh-oh." Her turn was coming up fast, and she wasn't even out of this dress yet. "Fay! You're run off your feet. Didn't Ermine say we'd get some help from the maids in the house?"

"I think so," Fay mumbled around a mouthful of pins. She was frantically stitching up the hem that Misty had stepped on and ripped.

"Right. I'm going for reinforcements." Sally left the room, closing the door behind her. After the craziness in the change room, the long, high corridor was as peaceful as a funeral parlour. And about as cozy, all snowy carpet and polished granite walls and stainless steel light fixtures.

From one end of the corridor came the sound of voices, music and applause. No doubt about it, Peter's designs were knocking their socks off! Sally walked in the other direction, her shoes soundless on the fleecy carpet. A staircase angled up at the end of the hall.

Where would you find a maid in a place like this? Upstairs or down? Sally looked up, and her eyebrows drew together. A slim figure in a red dress and hat was just passing out of sight up there above the stairwell railing.

Alys? Or Natasha? Whichever, she had no business upstairs. Ermine had made that very clear in a little talk before the show.

Sally glanced back toward the change room, then made a decision. If the thief was at work again, this could be a chance to catch her in the act. Technically, Peter had cut her from the case. But, she thought with a lift of her chin, it wasn't Peter who had called her in. Valerie had asked for help, and Sally hadn't delivered. As far as she was concerned, she was still investigating.

Her heart thudded. Taking a few deep breaths, she ran on tiptoe up the carpeted stairs. The hall above was softly lit and hung with pictures that looked as if they belonged in an art museum. Not that Alys was likely to lift one of those. Easily concealed bits of jewellery were probably more her target.

Silently Sally slipped along the hallway, trying the doors. Most were locked, but two opened. There was no sign of anyone anywhere, in the rooms or out.

She walked back to the stairwell and looked up. Could Alys have gone up to the third floor? Or had she gone down again by another way? There had to be more than one staircase in this huge place.

Movement flickered at the corner of her eye. She was just turning when someone grabbed the knotted scarf on the back of her neck and gave it a vicious twist. She choked. Her vision clouded.

Instinctively she jabbed backward with an elbow. Someone gasped behind her. Then a violent blow between the shoulder blades sent her tumbling down the stairs. Sparks burst in her head. Darkness swallowed her up.

Chapter 12

Thief!

"I THINK SHE'S coming out of it."

The darkness was clearing. The first thing she saw was Fay crouched beside her on the stairs, her face pinched with anxiety. Tasha, peering over her shoulder, broke into a smile as Sally's eyes opened.

On her other side, someone kept squeezing her hand. Sally turned her head and found Peter kneeling there, his eyes wide and black in a papery face.

"Don't look like that! I'm alive... I think." She tried to sit up, but sank down again. "Ow..." Pain zinged through her head.

"How is she?" Ermine's face appeared next to Peter's. She put both hands on Sally's cheeks and gazed into her eyes. Ermine's warm brown ones were strangely cold. "No sign of concussion, judging by the eyes, but you'd better get that checked. Detective Braun will drive you to the hospital."

"Braun's here?" Sally grimaced. "I wish I could swear who did this, but I can't."

Peter started to say something, but Ermine stood up and held up a hand. "Let's just get on with the show, okay? I know it's ruined, but at least Mrs. Creel is letting us finish. Fay, you're needed downstairs."

"But I can't leave Sal!"

"Fay, I'm all right!" To prove it, Sally pushed herself to a sitting position and managed a smile. "Away you go!" Fay gave her a doubtful look, then got up and ran downstairs.

"Now, Tasha—"

"I stay," Tasha said flatly.

Ermine gave her a hard look, then nodded. "You can help her get changed. Then I want her gone."

"This isn't fair," Peter said in a low voice.

"Maybe not. But you know we can't afford to be soft on a thief. Talk about bad press!"

"Thief?" Sally was confused. Maybe she was concussed after all. "You mean Braun has arrested Alys?"

"No," Ermine said. "He's going to arrest you."

Sally could only stare, flummoxed. Beside her, Tasha growled under her breath. The expression on Peter's face was unreadable. It could have disappointment, despair, or anything.

Ermine met Sally's eyes. "Natasha heard something back here and found you like this, halfway between the first and second floors. She called me, and I loosened your scarf so you could breathe better. Tucked inside the folds was a diamond tennis bracelet belonging to Mrs. Creel's daughter."

DETECTIVE BRAUN hadn't said much during the drive to the hospital, and Sally was still too shaken and confused to talk. Tasha was too furious.

By the time her checkup was complete, Sally's mind was clear. She found her escort in the waiting room and waved at them. Tasha looked a question.

"A little bruising and strain in the shoulder and a bump on the forehead, nothing serious. Also..." She met Braun's ironic eyes. "A bruise around my throat. The sort of mark that would have been caused by strangling."

45

He stood up. "May I?"

"See for yourself." She lifted her chin. After staring hard at her neck a moment, he stepped back.

"That scarf you were wearing, eh?"

"Right. And I never did that to myself! I didn't push myself downstairs, either."

Tasha stood with hands on hips, bristling. "I think some people owe Sally an apology. Starting with you!"

"Me?" He grinned at her. "You think I'm stupid? I never bought that clumsy frame."

Sally stared at him, surprised, then sighed. "But Ermine did. And I guess Mrs. Creel did too. And soon everybody in Knollvale..." Head down, she started walking toward the exit.

Braun caught her up. "I'll have a word with them. Meantime, you can tell me exactly what happened. We'll talk as we walk."

It didn't take long. By the time they were buckling their seatbelts in Braun's car, Sally was describing the flicker of movement just before the assault.

"I'd tried the door next to the stairs, and thought it was locked. She must have been holding the handle on the inside. Then slipped out when my back was turned."

"And," Tasha put in, "as soon as you were out cold, she ran down the stairs and hid the bracelet in your scarf. Then she 'discovered' you. It was Natasha who found you."

"We can't assume it was Natasha who attacked me." Sally shook her head, then winced and wished she hadn't. "It could have been Alys. With those identical outfits and the way they look, I just couldn't tell."

"There's my problem." Braun checked over his shoulder and backed out of the parking space. "I haven't a hope of charging either

46

of them if I don't know which it is."

"Suppose you grilled them?" Tasha clenched her fists and put on a mean-cop snarl. "You might learn something."

"Yeah, and I might just tip them off to be more careful, too."

"Well, there's one good thing." Sally gave the detective a grateful look. "At least now you agree with me that your case has more than one lead."

"Which case?" He turned onto the highway and accelerated. "If you mean the thefts, yeah. But I never ruled out the possibility that more than one girl was pilfering. If you mean the Mahon killing and the assault on Mrs. Engstrom, well... there's only one girl that's running scared."

Talk about stubborn! "Have you considered the idea that maybe Valerie didn't run?"

"Right," Tasha said. "Maybe she's been kidnapped, or... or..."

"You girls got any idea how hard it is to hide a body, let alone a live prisoner?" Braun sounded as if his patience was stretching thin again.

"They're still both possible, right?" Sally demanded.

"Just barely. And you got no evidence of anything like that." He gave her a knife-edged look. "And don't take that as a ticket to snoop! That sore head's a warning, Sally. Leave the detecting to the professionals. You got that?"

Chapter 13

Ermine Talks

SALLY HAD STOPPED simmering, just barely, by next morning. As her red Honda nosed along the curving drive to the farmhouse, she was reflecting that it hadn't taken Braun's patronizing tone of voice to goad her into action.

Whoever had pushed her down the stairs and planted the diamond bracelet had done that. Probably they hadn't really hoped the frame would stick. The attack had had one main purpose: to scare her off. It was a warning.

She twisted the wheel and swerved around the house to the back. The faceless *whoever* didn't know Sally Sharp very well. The attack had only made her more sure than ever that Valerie had been kidnapped and framed.

With all these unanswered questions chasing through her mind, nothing was going to keep Sally off the case. Not Peter Hewens, not Detective Braun, not *whoever*. She grabbed her bag with the notebook in it, bounced out of the car and strode to the house.

Ermine met her at the front door. "Stop right there," she snapped. "Braun phoned me. He told me you came here on Sunday to snoop, not to try out as a model — as I should have guessed. Don't expect me to like that."

"Well, I appreciate your agreeing to see me."

Ermine smiled coolly. "If I didn't, you'd think I had something to hide, wouldn't you?"

She waved Sally in, closed the door and led the way along the hall to a narrow wooden staircase. Over her shoulder she added, "I'm alone here today. We'll go up to my apartment."

Her living room was decorated in pale, bright blues and greens that echoed the summery colours outside the open windows. She sank onto a sofa and waved at an armchair. Then looked at Sally critically. "How's the head?"

"A bit sore." Sally touched the tender spot on her forehead. "I'll have a heck of a bruise."

"All your own fault. Nobody asked you to go snooping around in a stranger's house."

It hurt Sally that Ermine had turned cold, but she tried to shrug it off. It was a natural reaction; she couldn't expect anything else.

"I'd like you to tell me anything you can about Mrs. Mahon's murder," she began crisply, pulling her notebook from her bag. "Also anything you may have guessed about those thefts."

"Aren't the police handling that?" Ermine crossed her neatly trousered legs."I just want to put all that bad press behind me and get on with business."

"Bad press? Is that all it is to you?"

"You think I don't care?" Ermine suddenly flushed with anger. "You think it means nothing to me that a friend of mine is dead? Of course it matters!"

Sally cocked her head. "Friend of yours?"

"Kendra Mahon. You didn't know that, did you? We were class-mates together at TSFA fifteen years ago."

"TSFA?"

"The Toronto School of Fashion Arts."

"So you trained together?"

"Not only that, we were roommates for two years." Ermine flashed a wry smile. "So, am I a suspect?"

49

Sally smiled back. It was hard not to like Ermine, even now. "Not necessarily."

"Well, if I am, you'd better check out Peter too. He knew Kendra long before he met me. Didn't he tell you that?"

"No, he didn't." Just one more important fact Peter had forgotten to mention. He really hadn't been very open about anything, had he?

Ermine got up, crossed to the window and looked out at the woods. There was a hint of autumn gold in some of the leaves. Through gaps in the foliage Sally glimpsed the silvery grey of the ruined barn.

"In a way," Ermine said, "Kendra was the founder of Jones & Hewens. She was the person who brought Peter and me together. I was at a stage where I was tired of working for other people. I wanted my own label. But to get a new start I needed a partner, someone young and fresh."

"I was wondering about that. Isn't it unusual for a head designer to be as young as Peter?"

Ermine nodded. "The usual thing is to start as an apprentice. But after I met him and saw his designs, I could tell right away he had that spark I was looking for. So I gave him his chance." She smiled. "I've never regretted it."

Something was nagging at Sally. Then she had it. "I can't recall Kendra Mahon ever being mentioned as a designer. Did she work under another name?"

"Her birth name was Molson; she married a man named Mahon. But no, she never worked at all." Ermine bent to straighten a lacquered box on the coffee table. "Unless you think designing her own ball gowns is work."

Sally was perplexed. Ermine sank back onto the sofa and gave her a dry smile. "Kendra dropped out before she finished the program."

"Really? Why?"

Ermine flipped a hand. "You see, Sally, fashion design has a glamorous image, but there's a tremendous amount of work and stress involved. You need stamina and determination as well as talent. Kendra just couldn't hack the pressure and the workload. So she married a rich man and got out from under."

"How did she happen to meet Peter, then?"

"Oh, she kept up her ties with the school. Went to the exhibitions, met the students. She liked being with young people."

"Peter was a lot younger than her, right?"

"About fourteen years younger." Ermine got up again and prowled restlessly to the window. "Kendra was the kind of bored, wealthy woman who likes to collect protégés. It gave her a sense of accomplishment." Another ironic smile. "She liked to imagine that she was responsible for their successes. And Peter was a standout, obviously talented. So she collected him."

"They were close friends?" Sally made a note, then frowned. This shed a disturbing new light.

"You could say that. But — look." Ermine took a deep breath. "Kendra's dead now and you can't help her by raking all this up. Why don't we just drop it?"

"But suppose they quarrelled?"

"I wouldn't know anything about that." Ermine turned away abruptly. "You might as well go. I've got nothing more to say."

Sally suspected she had plenty to say. But it wouldn't do any good to try pressure. She put away her notebook, picked up her bag and walked to the stairs. Ermine followed her down.

"Oh, one more thing, Sally. About what happened last night." Ermine stood holding the front door open.

"Well?" Could this be an apology?

"Detective Braun talked to Mrs. Creel, and she won't lay charges. But she still thinks you're guilty. So do I."

"But that's—" Sally dropped her bag in shock.

Ermine cut her off. "The facts are against you. I'm guessing your mother has the police in her pocket."

"My mother! That's ridiculous!" Sally laughed incredulously.

Ermine gave her a tiny smile. "Lacey Sharp has quite a name in some quarters, as I'm sure you're aware. In business a good name is everything. Like mine. I can't afford to employ a suspected thief. You'll be paid for last night, but as of now you're not welcome at Jones & Hewens."

Chapter 14

Where is Valerie?

"THE NERVE!" Tasha's chicken bone thunked into the bottom of the cardboard carton. "Whenever I think of her saying that, I get so steamed — I wish I'd gone ahead and quit!"

At two o'clock that afternoon, Sally and Tasha were sitting on a stone retaining wall on the top of Rattlesnake Point. Here, a few miles east of Knollvale, belts of thick woodland and ripe cornfields rolled away below them into the haze of distance.

They were enjoying the view, soaking up the sun and eating take-out chicken as a reward for a morning of hard investigative legwork. They'd been tracking down and interviewing potential witnesses.

"I'm glad you didn't quit! You and Fay both." Sally brushed crumbs off her jeans. "We need the two of you inside Jones & Hewens, now that I'm out. Fay has already helped a lot."

"For all the good it did us," Tasha sighed.

"Oh, I think it did." Sally looked back over the day as she polished off a wing. Fay had phoned Sally about ten o'clock with a list of girls who had modelled for Jones & Hewens in the past season, besides Alys and Natasha Krug. All of them were students at Knollvale High School, and all were acquainted with either Sally, Tasha or Fay. That made it easier to get in touch with them and ask questions.

"But none of them could tell us a thing!" Tasha groused.

Sally poked her playfully on the arm. "Did you expect them to pour out details about the murder?"

"Well, no. But all they could do was snipe at Alys. And go on

53

about her flashy wardrobe."

"Right." Sally looked thoughtful. "That gold watch, and those two-hundred-dollar boots. And a couple of the girls mentioned that her family's just barely scraping along. Makes you wonder where Alys's money comes from, doesn't it?"

"Not from her measly salary at Jones & Hewens, that's for sure." The amount of Alys's salary was another item Fay had dug out from computerized records.

"I wonder if those girls were trying to get something across to us?" Sally tapped her lip with a chicken bone.

"If they knew anything against Alys, wouldn't they say so?"

"Would they?" Sally dropped the last bone into a carton and found a tissue to clean her greasy fingers. "Didn't something strike you about the way they looked? And talked?"

Tasha took the carton and tossed it neatly into the nearby garbage bin. "I noticed they didn't really want to talk. Especially when you mentioned Dylan."

"You got it. I was watching their eyes, and I'm sure of it. They were scared!"

Tasha thought back. "You know, you're right? Those girls were scared silly. I guess that tells us something."

"All the same, it doesn't prove either Alys or Dylan's a killer. All we've got is a very strong suspicion that Alys has been stealing things from clients' houses to pay for her expensive swag, so she can fit in with Dylan's crowd. And Val may have been a threat because she knew this: maybe she'd seen something, and she might have threatened to tell Peter."

"We'd already guessed all that. And you've told the police."

"Yes, and I've got a feeling nothing will change Braun's mind, not until he sees another body. Val's." Sally shivered.

"Don't say it!" Tasha gazed out over the mellow countryside. "I know he said it would be hard to hide a body, but just look at those thick woods. Dozens of bodies could be buried in there, and nobody'd ever find them."

Sally followed her gaze. It was true. If Val was dead, she might never be found.

She raised her chin stubbornly. "I have to keep believing she's alive. And you can't just stash a live person in the woods. Think, Tash! If Dylan and Alys kidnapped her, where could she be?"

Tasha pulled her legs up and crossed them under her on the stone wall. "Well... not in or around Alys's house, anyway. The girls said it was a tiny place. On the other hand, the Thatchers' place is huge."

"Y-yes... A big house with lots of land." Sally shook her head. "But it's right in town, and there'd be people around, servants probably, inside and out. It would be really hard to hide a person there and expect nobody to notice. *Maybe* you could do it, but..."

Suddenly she sat up straight. "Of course!" She jumped off the wall and did a little shuffling dance in the grass.

"What's this?" Tasha jumped down after her.

Sally pulled out her cellphone. "Just let me get at the internet. Then I'll tell you if it's a live hunch or a dead end!"

Chapter 15

A Fresh Plot

"SO ANOTHER HUNCH works out." Tasha drove her paddle into the current and the canoe glided in beside the pier. "Sal, we're on a roll!"

"So long as we've got the right house." Sally shaded her eyes against the late afternoon sun. "From the back, it's hard to tell."

"It's the one, all right," Tasha said confidently. "I can tell by the roof line."

Locating the Thatchers' summer place was easy: the address was on Canada 411, just as Sally had hoped. Getting there was just a thirty-minute drive south.

Getting into the house turned out to be the hard part. The property was protected on the front and sides by a high iron fence and security cameras — no surprise there. But through the trees Sally had glimpsed the sparkle of water, and guessed the property backed onto the Grand River.

A mile farther on they found a road leading down to a riverside village that catered to vacationers and picnickers. They parked, rented a canoe and started paddling back along the shore.

Sally shook her head as they climbed out onto the pier. "It can't be this easy. If the fence was rigged with alarms, the house will be too." She stared up at it.

They had come this far on the gamble that the summer place might not be in use, this close to the start of the new school semester. If they'd lost the gamble — if the place looked lived-in and busy —

then obviously Valerie wouldn't be hidden there, and they'd have called it a loss and gone home.

But the property seemed to be deserted. All the same, Sally didn't like the idea of breaking into someone's home. Still less did she like the idea of being caught, and charged with break-and-enter. But if Valerie was being held prisoner in there...

"Hey, look!" Tasha pointed. "I think they're having the place painted."

A van with a decorating company logo on its side was parked near a door in the rear of the house.

"That would explain why none of the family are in," Sally said. "Paint fumes."

As the two girls watched from behind a clump of cedars, the door opened and two men came out carrying a ladder between them. They tied it on top of the van and went back into the house.

"Looks like they're about to knock off." Tasha was whispering, although the men couldn't have heard her across that expanse of lawn.

Sally bit the side of her lip, then decided. "We go in now."

"Now! But—"

"They'll lock up after themselves if we wait any longer. This could be our only chance to get inside without being seen. And without actually breaking in."

Tasha took a steadying breath. "Okay. And if anybody spots us?"

"We say we're lost."

Sally set off briskly across the lawn. Nobody seemed to be watching from the dozens of windows, but she had a queasy feeling that at any moment someone might look out and spot them. Detouring around a freshly dug flower bed, she reached the back door behind the van and slipped inside. Tasha was close at her heels.

They were in a small room with raincoats hanging from hooks along one wall. Rubber boots stood with croquet mallets in a corner.

Voices and footsteps sounded nearby. Sally looked around wildly for cover. "Quick!" she hissed.

Seconds later she was crouching behind a drapery of raincoats, elbow to elbow with Tasha. The coats smelled of rubber and mildew. She hoped she wouldn't sneeze. She also hoped the men would be too busy to notice how the coats bulged.

Feet scuffed by. The door creaked as it swung open, then a voice called out: "Wait a second till I get this door locked!"

A slam, a pause, then the click of a bolt. Sally stayed perfectly still and listened. After a minute of silence, a motor revved up and growled away into the distance.

They crawled out from behind the coats. Tasha stood up stretched. "I can't believe it! We've got the house all to ourselves!"

"That's what I'm afraid of."

IT TOOK THEM TWO HOURS to be sure. They began with the attic and worked their way down through the second and first floors to the cellar. They poked and peered into every cranny and cupboard. They shouted, they knocked on walls, they listened.

By the time they were finished, the sun had set.

"I was afraid of this," Sally said glumly as they found their way through the dim rooms to the back door. "With the painters having the run of the house, it wasn't likely Dylan would have tried hiding Valerie here."

"No, but we had to look." Tasha turned the latch and they stepped out into the twilight. She added, "We can't lock up. Those guys will get in trouble."

"Oh, I don't think—" Sally had started off across the darkened lawn toward the pier, then stumbled into a bed of soft earth: the freshly dug flowerbed. She fell forward. Her hands sank in up to the wrists.

A sudden notion chilled her. She scrambled back off the flower bed, scrubbing earth off her hands onto her jeans. Then she stood up and walked all around the patch of newly turned earth, tracing its shape and size. A spade had been driven into the turf nearby.

Tasha took a step back and pointed. "Sally, could... No. It couldn't be... Could it?"

"Uh... It's probably just a flower bed."

But all the other flower beds were neat crescents and squares and circles full of roses or chrysanthemums or asters. This was a crude oblong, not quite six feet by two.

Just the right size for one slender girl.

Chapter 16

Knife

"BUT WHY would they leave it uncovered like this?" Tasha whispered. "It's so obvious!"

"Maybe they were planning to come back and plant flowers in it." Sally felt sick. She looked at the spade, took a deep breath and pulled it out of the ground.

"W-wait a minute." In the dusk, Tasha's face looked white. "Shouldn't we call the police?"

"And suppose there's nothing here?"

"I get you. Braun would throw the book at us. And after that he'd never listen to us again."

Sally nodded. She looked at Tasha, looked at the spade in her hands, and took a couple of deep, steadying breaths. *Get it over with!* With a thrust she sent the spade deep into the soft soil.

The first spadeful brought up nothing but earth. She tried in a different place. Still nothing. Then Tasha took over and probed in the middle of the patch. She froze and looked up.

"There's something here."

Sally swallowed, and prayed. *Please, let it be a rock.*

Tasha used the edge of the spade very delicately to scrape away some of the earth. The thing she uncovered was white and the size of a hand. "Oh—!" She dropped the spade and jumped back.

Reluctantly, Sally bent to look closer. In the dusk the thing was hard to see, but it wasn't a hand. She let out the breath she'd been holding. It looked like a root or tuber of some kind. She picked it up.

60

"Let's try again."

Tasha spaded up more tubers. Then she stopped, leaned on the spade and burst out laughing. "Asparagus!" she whooped.

"Asparagus?" Sally made a face at the thing in her hand. "We've dug up a bed of asparagus roots?"

"And some poor gardener probably slaved over it. Sal, we're going great guns today!"

Sally dropped the root and brushed dirt off her hands. She felt as if a twenty-pound weight had lifted from her shoulders.

"I've never been more glad to be wrong!"

The girls giggled helplessly as they pushed the roots back into the earth as gently as they could and carefully covered them over.

"There," Sally said with a final pat. "I hope there's a bumper crop!"

Out of nowhere, a dazzling beam of light caught her full in the face.

"Well, isn't this sweet!"

Sally stood up, shielding her eyes with her hand. She could just glimpse two big shapes in the darkness behind the light. The husky, jeering voice wasn't familiar, but she already knew she wouldn't like its owner.

"Hey, those are the two from the mall!" said a lighter voice. There was a clinking sound, as if a case full of bottles had been set down on the grass.

"That's right, Eddie." There was menace in the mocking tone. "Hey, here's an idea! Let's ask Sally and Tasha to join us. How about it, girls?"

Sally smiled, still shading her eyes. "Some other time, perhaps," she said lightly. Meanwhile she was trying to remember exactly in what direction the pier lay. They might have to run for it. She could hear Tasha's tense, quick breathing close beside her.

"Tasha?" burst out the second boy. "That's no girl. That's the gorilla that knocked me down!"

"Yeah, and I'll do it again if you don't take that light out of my eyes," Tasha said grimly.

The first voice rumbled with laughter. Sally had a good idea who he was by now. "What are you doing here, Dylan? Having a little party where your parents won't know about it?"

"This is my house. I don't have to answer to any jumped-up snoop. You're too big for your boots, Sally Sharp." Dylan's voice turned sly. "Hey, ever think you might get *too* sharp? Watch out you don't get so sharp you cut yourself, Sally." He laughed again. "Like this."

They heard a metallic click. Then a long, bright shape moved into the flashlight beam. A knife blade. Sally tingled all over as the adrenaline started flowing.

If only that light wasn't blinding her! Taking a quick glance back, she saw the spade stuck in the earth just beyond arm's reach.

"Put the knife away," she said evenly. "It isn't cool to play with pointy things."

"It isn't cool to trespass, either." There was a snarl in Dylan's voice. "Not on Thatcher land."

She poised, her eyes on the knife blade. When he made his move it was so sudden, he almost took her by surprise. The blade flashed, then a big shape was leaping at her through the beam.

Sally lunged sideways, grabbed the spade and swung it — not at the knife, but at the flashlight. There was a *crack* and the light went out.

A hand closed on her wrist and something whammed the side of her head, knocking her off balance. *Dylan — fighting dirty.* She used her grip on his arm to stay on her feet and swing around him, at the same time chopping sharply down on his forearm with the side of her hand. He grunted with pain and let go. A few yards away someone else yelled, then a body thudded on the grass.

"Tash!"

"Right here!"

Now that the light was out, they could see the lake glimmering in the distance. They raced to the pier. Yelling voices grew faint behind them.

"Sounds like Eddie's getting chewed out for losing the light," Tasha laughed breathlessly as she scrambled into the canoe.

"What did you do to him?" Sally grabbed a paddle and they sent the canoe skimming away from the pier.

"Decked him again, that's all. I'm afraid Eddie and I are just never going to get along!"

Chapter 17

Girl on the Run

"WELL, WE LEARNED one thing from that," Sally said as the red Honda pulled in at Tasha's house. "It proves Dylan is vicious enough to have attacked Mrs. Engstrom or kidnapped Valerie, or both."

"Too bad it doesn't prove he actually did." Tasha paused half in and half out of the front seat. "Sal, I've got to get moving. I've got about forty minutes to shower, dress and get over to the Knollvale Businesswomen's Club. That's where we're staging tonight's show."

"Keep an eye on Alys, okay? And, Tasha..."

"Yes?"

"Be careful. I have a feeling she's as dangerous as Dylan."

Sally drove home, washed off the day's grime, brushed her hair and tied it into a ponytail, and changed into clean chinos and T-shirt.

In the kitchen she found Brandon digging into a bowl of chicken noodle soup and a triple-layer grilled cheese sandwich. She sighed as she sat down at the table. "Any chance I can share your sandwich?"

Bran looked up from the *Popular Science* magazine he was reading. "Too lazy to make your own, eh?"

"Too tired. I've had a busy day."

"Busy snooping? That takes energy?"

"Bran..."

"Oh, all right. Here." He pushed the plate toward her. "Take half. Nobody can say I don't pamper my little sister."

"Mm. Thanks." She bit and chewed, but after a few bites put the sandwich down and pushed the plate back.

64

"What, you don't like my cooking?"

"Not that." She sank her head in her hands. "I just feel so frustrated! This case is going nowhere. If only Mom were here!"

"This 'case.' For Pete's sake, kid, grow up!"

"That's exactly what I'm doing! In case you haven't noticed!"

Brandon snorted. Sally got up, went to the refrigerator for a glass of milk, then retreated to her bedroom. Opening her laptop, she began working out a list of suspects and motives in connection with the thefts, assault and murder. It was a very short list.

"Alys and Dylan," Sally muttered, tapping the screen with a fingertip. "But where's my proof?"

Her cellphone played a chiming tune: the theme from *The Twilight Zone*. It was Fay. "Sal, I'm calling from the Businesswomen's Club. This could be nothing, but it looks suspicious. I've never seen anybody move that fast!"

Sally sat up straight. "What is it?"

"Well, the girls got paid tonight for their two modelling stints. Ermine actually gave them cash, can you believe that? Anyway, Natasha Krug just grabbed her envelope and ran out of here as if somebody'd lit a fire under her!"

"Natasha?" Sally sank back onto her bed, disappointed. "Fay, she's probably just going home. Maybe she had a bus to catch."

"She did: I was watching from a window on the second floor. Only, she took the southbound bus. You know the route it takes. Her home's in the other direction. Tasha said to tell you she'll follow the bus in her car and see where Natasha goes. She'll give you a buzz if anything happens."

"And what's Alys doing?"

"She's still in the change room." Fay added, "I was watching them both. Alys is cool as ever, but Natasha's been on pins and needles all evening. Sal, is it possible we've been suspecting the wrong sister?"

"Anything's possible. Thanks, Fay. You're right, it could be important."

Sally pocketed her phone and ran downstairs. It wasn't exactly a breakthrough, but the way this case was going, she couldn't afford to pass up any lead, no matter how slight.

FIFTEEN MINUTES later Sally edged her Honda into a space in a line of light traffic behind Tasha's aging Ford. Just ahead was the southbound bus. Tasha caught sight of her in the rearview mirror and made the OK sign with her right hand. So Natasha hadn't got off yet.

Two blocks farther on, in a district of seedy second-hand stores and pawnbrokers, a slim blond girl got off the bus and scurried along the street. Sally pulled in to the curb and got out. When Tasha joined her the two girls walked briskly along, a safe distance behind Natasha.

"Stay close to the store fronts," Sally said. "Pretend we're window shopping."

"I wish she'd picked a nicer part of town. This area's kinda scary, especially at night."

A couple of rough-looking men stared at them in passing. Sally strode on confidently, knowing the best way to stay out of trouble was not to look like a victim.

"She's slowing down," Tasha muttered.

Sally slowed down too, and the two girls crowded into a doorway. Then they peered out. Half a block ahead, Natasha stood staring into a lit window. She hovered hesitantly. Then, as if she'd suddenly made up her mind, she darted into the shop.

When Tasha and Sally reached the spot, they found a grimy store front with a grille-protected window. The chipped gold letters on the glass read: S. J. MONDELL — WATCHES AND JEWELLERY BOUGHT AND SOLD.

The window was so dirty that it was almost impossible to see into the shop — which might be exactly how the shopkeeper liked it, Sally figured. After some searching, she found a relatively clean spot and put her eye to it.

"She's in there, all right." Sally moved aside so Tasha could see.

A wizened, balding man was scowling across a high counter at Natasha. They couldn't see her face or hear what she was saying, but she was leaning forward, one hand outstretched as if pleading. Then she pulled something from her shoulder bag and tried to push it into the man's hand.

"She's trying to sell him something," Tasha whispered. "Only he doesn't want to buy."

Sally shook her head in disbelief. "So Natasha's the thief. Not Alys! I've been wrong all along!"

Chapter 18

Hot Bling

"I'VE GOT TO hear what they're saying!" Sally moved to the door.

Tasha was right behind her. "If it's anything criminal, they'll shut up as soon as they see us."

"Then we won't let them see us."

Sally opened the door a crack. She had a glimpse of the man's face and the back of Natasha's head. Then he half turned toward the back of the store, as if talking to someone in the rear.

It was the only chance they were likely to get. Sally pushed the door open a few more inches and slipped in. At once she stepped behind a bay of shelving that screened her from the counter. She found herself standing in a narrow canyon lined with shelves holding used clocks, stereos and televisions.

Tasha was beside her a second later and the door closed noiselessly. They stood still and listened.

"Please," Natasha was saying, "I promise I'll give you more in a week. I'd pay it all right now, but this is all I've got!" Her voice quivered. She sounded on the verge of tears.

"Look, kid. I don't take time payments and I don't have no layaway plan. This ain't Sears!"

"Could— could you at least hold them for a week? Not sell them? I'll buy them back then, I swear it!"

"Didn't you get my drift?" he said gruffly. "You want them earrings, you pay me what I paid for them, plus my markup, and do it now. I got a living to make!"

Sally met Tasha's eyes. She had an idea of what was going on here.

Relying on Tasha to follow her lead, she wandered along the shelves of electronics and out at the end nearest to the counter. "No, I don't think so," she said vaguely.

Turning around, she found Natasha staring at her in shock. The storekeeper scowled suspiciously. "Where'd you come from? I didn't see you come in."

"I guess you were busy." Sally smiled mildly at him. "We were looking for a good used TV, but looks like I'm in the wrong place."

Natasha slipped past her and barged out the door. It slammed behind her. Sally glanced after her indifferently, then back at the rows of second-hand appliances.

The man gave them a snaggle-toothed grin, apparently meant to be a winning smile. "If you don't see what you want, girls, I can find it for you. Gimme a day, two at the most. What was the model you was after?"

"Oh, come on." Tasha sniffed and took Sally's arm. "Buy new, I always say. Fewer problems."

"Maybe you're right." Sally waved airily and the two girls walked out.

"I'll just bet he could find it for us," Tasha said with a laugh. "Off the back of a truck!"

"You got it. He's a crook, I'm sure of it. I hope he doesn't know we know." Sally looked around in all directions and spotted a figure dashing across the street. "Come on!"

Natasha put on a burst of speed, but Tasha went flat out and caught her before she'd run another half block. When Sally got there, Natasha was huddled against a restaurant window and choking back tears.

"Hey, it's all right!" Sally slipped an arm around her. "We can help you."

"I don't know what you're talking about!" The younger girl pushed her away.

"Oh, yes, you do. But you're not going to save your sister this way. You can't keep bailing her out of trouble, even if you could afford to."

Natasha looked frightened. "You're — you're wrong! This is nothing to do with Alys. I— I sold some of my own jewellery, a — a locket my mother gave me, and I was trying to buy it back. That's all!"

"A locket? The man said earrings, didn't he?"

"Oh — leave me alone!" A bus roared up the street behind them. Natasha darted around Sally, sprinted for the bus as it came to the stop, and leaped aboard.

"What now?" Tasha asked as they walked back to their cars. "Seems like another dead end."

"I don't think so. Let's go to Fay's place and talk this over."

"SO NATASHA was trying to buy back the stolen jewellery." Fay swirled the diet cola in her glass.

"It looks that way, doesn't it?" Sally tucked her feet under her on the sofa. "She was trying to persuade the man not to sell some earrings till she could scrape together the money for them. She was offering her modelling pay as a first instalment."

Tasha stretched and yawned. "And all that doesn't make much sense, does it? Not if she stole the earrings in the first place."

"But it does make sense if someone else stole them. And if Natasha was trying to protect that someone." Sally yawned too. It had been a long and exhausting day.

"And who would she want to protect but her own sister?" Fay put in.

Sally nodded. "She must be terrified Alys will be caught. Maybe she has some hope of helping her break this habit of theft — or break free of that expensive lifestyle of hers."

"If she is, she's kidding herself," Tasha said.

"Maybe. But it's what a sister would do." Sally sighed. "Natasha will be devastated if Alys is nailed. So will their parents, I bet."

She wished it wasn't necessary to go to Detective Braun with the information they'd gained tonight. But she knew she had no choice.

"Sally," Tasha said, "I know what you mean. But if Alys isn't stopped, she'll just get in deeper."

"Maybe getting arrested will knock some sense into her," Fay added.

"You're both right." Sally yawned again and pushed herself up off the sofa. "I'll call Braun first thing in the morning."

Chapter 19

Alys Arrested

AT NOON the next day, the three friends were sitting in a waiting room at Knollvale Police Station. Sally and Tasha had made their report verbally and had signed typed statements.

They had decided not to mention yesterday's encounter with Dylan Thatcher. Braun couldn't be expected to overlook Sally's sneaking into somebody's house, even if the door wasn't locked. Besides, there was still nothing that positively connected Dylan to either the thefts or the murders.

Tasha shifted uncomfortably on the hard plastic chair. "I'm getting stiff, sitting here and doing nothing. How much longer will we have to wait?"

"This is it, I think." Sally nodded at an inner door that had just opened. Braun came out with a file of papers in his hand. He was smiling, for a change. It brightened up his whole appearance.

He stopped beside Sally's chair. "I guess I owe you one, young lady. Thanks to you, we've tied up one end of this case."

"Only one end? Which?"

"The thefts." He looked grim again. "She denies anything to do with the Mahon and Engstrom cases and we can't shake her on those."

"Were we right about that jeweller?" Tasha asked.

"Right on the button. He's as crooked as they come. Following up on your tip, we recovered several pieces of jewellery: all the stuff that was stolen from the houses where Jones & Hewens held their fashion shows."

Tasha grinned. "Good. Did you arrest him?"

"What d'you think?" Braun looked disgusted. "The guy put on a big innocent act. Said he had no idea the stuff was hot. All we could do was warn him. The main thing is, after we showed him a bunch of photos, he identified Alys Krug as the girl who sold him the jewellery."

"Something's been bothering me," Sally said. "It may be nothing, but... that expensive gold watch she wears. Was there anything like it on the list of stolen items?"

"Uh-uh. I noticed that watch too and found out where she bought it. It's hers, all right."

"Hm. And do you think the money she got from that fence would cover the cost of the watch?"

"Nowhere near." Braun looked at her sharply. "What are you getting at?"

"That she must have got the money from somewhere else. But where?" Sally looked up as another inner door opened and voices drifted out. "That sounds like Peter."

A moment later he walked out, followed by Ermine. Spotting the three girls he stopped, frowned at them, then strode out the front door.

"Good grief!" Tasha flung up her hands. "Anybody'd think he didn't want Valerie to be cleared!"

"Right!" Sally looked at Braun. "That reminds me. How is Mrs. Engstrom?"

"Still hanging on. The doctor's surprised. Must be a tough old bird, that lady."

"Oh, good. But is she..."

"No. Still in a coma. If she ever comes out of it, we'll get proof of Valerie's guilt, I hope."

"Or her innocence!" Sally flashed back at him.

"We'll see," Braun said shortly. He turned on his heel and walked away. As he left, Ermine crossed the room to where the girls were sitting and held out her hand.

"Apologies," she said quietly. "I was wrong."

Sally shook her hand warmly. "Accepted!"

Fay scooted over to make room, and Ermine sat down between them. "I'm glad the real thief is caught. I'm just sorry it had to be Alys. My best model!"

"What will happen to her now?"

"She'll likely get probation. It's a first charge, and she's entitled to her chance. She's to be released into her parents' custody until the case comes up in court." Ermine sighed. "But naturally I had to fire her."

"That's understandable," Tasha said pointedly. "You fired Sally just on suspicion."

"So I did." Ermine rose gracefully from her chair, turned and gave Sally a wry smile. "If you want your job back, dear, it's yours. I'd be glad to have you."

Sally rose to face her. After a moment's thought, she smiled and shook her head. "Thanks. But no, I'm pretty sure modelling's not for me."

"That's a shame. You have a flair for it." Ermine shrugged, turned away and walked out.

Fay grabbed Sally's arm. "I can't believe it! You just tossed away the most glamorous job ever!"

"Maybe so. It's just that..." Sally frowned as she sat down again. "I don't know what it is. I admire Ermine, but there's something a bit... well, off-putting about her. Something cold. I don't think I want to work for her."

"Well, if it was me—"

"Hey, look." Tasha silenced Fay with a poke in the ribs. "Here comes Alys."

Not just Alys. The whole Krug family was there. Natasha walked in the rear, holding the hand of a gaunt middle-aged woman. On her other side walked a greying man who was twisting a battered feed store cap in his hands. Natasha's face was tear-streaked.

Sally's heart sank when she saw them. She could imagine what they were feeling. But she still wouldn't have gone back on turning Alys in.

The only member of the family who didn't look stricken was Alys herself. She strutted in front, tossing her hair and sweeping the room with a defiant smile.

When she caught sight of Sally she came to an abrupt halt. Their eyes locked. Then Alys smiled mockingly and strolled on toward the door. On the way she made a detour that brought her past the line of chairs. Sally looked up at her warily.

Alys bent close and breathed a whisper that nobody else could hear. "Better keep looking over your shoulder, Sally Snoop. Or one of these days you're going to end up in an alley. All cut to pieces!"

Chapter 20

Warning

NEXT MOMENT Alys was on her way out the door, smirking. Sally shivered, then tried to shrug off the uneasy feeling. She'd been threatened before, usually without much effect. All the same, so much venom was disturbing.

It was obvious neither Tasha nor Fay had heard the hate-filled whisper. Sally decided to leave it at that.

As they left the air-conditioned police station, the strong sunlight and thick humidity fell on them like a blanket. "Oof!" said Fay. "You know what would go good right now? A nice, cold double-scoop ice cream cone. Let's go to the Creamery!"

"I'm up for that," Sally agreed. "Let's forget about this miserable case for an hour!"

"Um..." Tasha touched her arm. "Easier said than done. Look there!"

Peter Hewens was leaning against a hydro pole at the curb, arms crossed, glowering at Sally from under his dark brows.

"What a babe!" Fay muttered. "Don't I wish he'd stare at me like that!"

"I don't," Sally muttered back. "He's not flirting. Far from it."

Peter didn't smile as they crossed the sidewalk. He nodded at Fay and Tasha, then focused on Sally. "I need a word with you alone."

Sally looked at her friends. Fay winked impishly and took Tasha's arm. "We'll be at the Creamery, across the street. You be good, now!" They ran off.

76

Peter looked grimly back at Sally. "This won't take long. Didn't I tell you to drop the investigation?"

"You did. I didn't."

"Then you should have!" he snapped. "You have no right to do this on your own. I want you to stop this silly game right now!"

Sally was nettled. "You're not my boss, and I don't play games, especially when people's lives are involved." She took a quick breath. "But you do — play games. How *dare* you lie to me?"

"Lie?" He glared. "I never lied!"

"Oh yeah? Well then, you did the next thing to it: you kept back information. Important information."

"Like what?"

"Like the fact that it was you who found Mrs. Mahon's body." She watched his face for a reaction, but he only looked grimmer. "And the fact that you and she were good friends. You left me with the impression that you'd hardly met her."

"What does it matter?" He swung away abruptly and started walking fast along the street. Sally kept pace with him.

"It matters because it makes me wonder what else you're hiding. Like, whether you were on good terms with her at the end, or not? Did you quarrel?"

"That's irrelevant." He stopped by a parked car, a butter-yellow Mustang, and got out his keys. "Kendra could be infuriating at times, but that doesn't mean—" He stopped, keys in hand. A look of angry astonishment washed over his face. His black eyes snapped. "What are you accusing me of?"

"Not a thing. I'm asking you to be honest. What was your real reason for calling me off the case?"

He was too angry to listen. "Did I kill Kendra, is that it? Did I bash poor old Mrs. Engstrom on the head, just to get Val in trouble?

And Val, what about her? Did I kidnap my own sister? Why? What sense does any of it make?"

He was so fierce, Sally took a step backward. Then a flush of anger heated her cheeks. She darted forward and caught his sleeve as he started around the car to the driver's side.

"Wait just a minute! There's something you've forgotten. You're not the one who first asked me to investigate, remember? That was Val. She asked for my help and I'm not going to let her down, even if you are!"

He stared at her with a look so intense, she wondered if the strain of Val's disappearance had unhinged him a little.

"Has it occurred to you," he said quietly, "that a woman has been killed? And another nearly?"

"And a girl disappeared. Yes, I noticed," she said evenly.

His mouth tightened. "Then you must realize there's a lot at stake here. For your own sake, Sally, I'm telling you to back off!"

"That sounds very much like a threat." Her blue eyes held his dark ones.

"Call it a warning."

Chapter 21
The Case Against Peter

"WELL, THAT LOOKED interesting," Fay commented as Sally slid into a chair beside her. "We were watching you through the window. Come on, spill!"

Sally picked up the mint-chocolate-chip waffle cone they had ordered for her and licked off the bits that were beginning to melt. After getting the drips under control she said, "I don't know whether he was threatening me or trying to protect me."

She gave them the gist of her conversation with Peter. Tasha was frowning before she finished. "It strikes me he's acting as if he has something to hide, Sally, and he doesn't want you digging it up. Do you think you can trust him?"

Sally sighed and slurped at her cone. "I'm not sure."

"Don't tell me Peter ever hurt anyone!" Fay flared up.

Tasha laughed. "Simmer down! Just because he's a babe doesn't mean he's the salt of the earth."

"It doesn't make him a monster, either! Hasn't it hit you, either of you, there could be another reason why Peter's being so mysterious?"

"Don't just tantalize us," Sally said.

Fay bent forward over the table. "He might be protecting Valerie!"

"You mean..." Sally set her cone down in its cardboard holder. "You mean suppose Val is guilty after all. Suppose she did kill Mrs. Mahon and lashed out at the old lady. And Peter's hiding her?" She set her teeth. "That's still pretty bad on his part."

"Of course it is." Fay shook back her hair impatiently. "But at least it's understandable. Maybe he hates what she did but he can't bear the idea of losing her. I mean, they'd put her in a juvenile detention centre, right? That's like a jail for kids. And she's his little sister!"

"Try it the other way around," Tasha suggested. "Suppose he quarreled with Kendra Mahon and accidentally killed her."

Fay waved her hands fanwise. "Too many loose ends. How would you tie in Val's disappearance, and why would Peter rob and assault old Mrs. Engstrom?"

"I wonder," Sally said slowly, "whether we're trying to connect too many things to one person. Maybe Mrs. Mahon's death had nothing to do with anything else."

"Here's what I think." Tasha held up a hand and ticked the points off on her fingers. "Peter killed Mrs. Mahon, maybe by accident. Alys did all the stealing. Dylan kidnapped Val and assaulted the old lady, to help Alys."

"Peter's no killer!" Fay said indignantly. "I'll bet if you were to watch him, Sally, you'd find out where Valerie's hiding. He'd have to take food to her, for one thing, because wherever she is, she can't go out, right?"

"I don't like the idea of spying on him." Sally shoved her cone away. "I like him too much. But I can't just let the case drop. There are too many questions without answers. Like, that gold watch of Alys's..."

"You've mentioned it before," Fay said curiously. "Why is it such a problem?"

"Because she couldn't have paid for it by selling those bits of stolen jewellery. Even combined with her modelling salary."

80

"In other words..." Tasha began slowly.

"Who's paying her large gobs of money, and for what?"

For another minute the only sound at the table was the meditative crunching of the last bits of waffle cone. Then Fay said: "What are we talking about here? Blackmail?"

"It's just an idea." Sally pulled her bag toward her. "I've got to go and see Peter now. I have to find out what he's keeping to himself."

"Then we'd better go with you," Tasha said. "It may not be safe for you to see him alone."

"No, you don't. He may not talk if there's a crowd."

"But—"

"Come on, Tash. Since when did I get helpless? Besides, you know I never take stupid risks."

Tasha gave in grudgingly and gave Fay a lift home, since neither of them was needed at Jones & Hewens today. Sally used her cellphone to call Peter's home, but all she got was an answering machine. She realized then that he'd probably gone to the studio, since it was still mid-afternoon.

When she unlocked the Honda and climbed in, she found a surprise on the front seat. A folded sheet of paper. She unfolded it and stared.

In block capitals was printed: KEEP LOOKING OVER YOUR SHOULDER, SALLY SNOOP!

Chapter 22

A Cry for Help

HER FIRST IMPULSE was to crumple the paper and toss it in the nearest trash bin. Instead she placed it carefully in the glove compartment. Detective Braun might find the note interesting.

The one thing that really bothered her was how Alys had bypassed the car's locked doors. She — or Dylan — must have the skills of a car thief.

"Thanks, Alys," Sally said aloud. "I do need a reminder to be careful, from time to time." She turned around, knelt up and peered into the back seat. Empty.

Then, as she glanced through the rear window, she found herself looking into the face of the driver in the car parked behind hers. It was a white Corvette, and the driver was Dylan Thatcher. He sent her a sly, closed-mouth smile.

"Oh, brother!" Exasperated, Sally belted herself in and pulled away from the curb. The white Corvette swerved out after her.

Dylan turned out to be a better driver than she would have guessed. After miles of quick turns, doubling back and weaving through traffic, he was still on her tail. Every time she looked into the rearview mirror there he was, smirking back at her.

Half an hour of this game had Sally fuming. She considered ignoring him and driving straight to the studio, but decided against it. That stretch of highway was just too lonely and the farmhouse too isolated.

She could always give up and go home. But catching sight of that smirk one more time decided her. No way was she letting Dylan win!

The next turnoff was into the mall parking lot. *I could lose him in the mall,* Sally thought. Then: *No, I can do better than that.* She drove into the parking lot, found a spot close to the entrance, and walked in.

After making a brief call on her cellphone, she walked through the mall to the back entrance, making sure Dylan wasn't anywhere in sight. As she'd hoped, instead of following her in, he must still be out front watching her car, waiting for her to return.

Fifteen minutes later, Tasha trotted up to the back entrance and dropped a set of keys into Sally's hand. Sally laughed and handed over the keys to the Honda. "Thanks, pal. You'll find it out front, near the doors."

Tasha grinned back. "Mine's next to the lamp standard, way in the back near the exit road. I'll give you ten minutes to get away and then I'll stroll out there and make his eyes pop."

With a cheerful wave, Sally was on her way again. It occurred to her that she'd just added more fuel to Dylan's grudge against her, but that didn't worry her. Much.

SALLY PARKED Tasha's car under a silver birch tree and got out. As always, once the car engine was shut off, the stillness of this spot spread out like an overflowing pond. The wide belt of woods between the old farmhouse and the highway acted as a baffle.

It struck her now that the baffle would work just as well the other way around. Nobody passing within a hundred yards of the place would hear voices.

She looked toward the ruined barn, a corner of its roof just visible through the trees. "What a perfect place to hide," she murmured half aloud. "Nobody would have the faintest idea you were there."

Not unless you tried to draw attention to yourself by yelling and screaming. And maybe not even then.

She hesitated, glancing back at the house. Then she began walking slowly through the woods toward the barn. If I don't search it, she told herself, I'll always wonder.

She was still within sight of the house when a sound came that froze her to the spot. The rustle of disturbed brush and scuffed leaves died, and she strained her ears.

For a moment there was no sound but the sighing of wind through the trees. Then... yes, there it was again: very faint and thin, as if calling from a distance. But it was unmistakably a human voice.

Help... please help me...

It was Valerie's voice!

Chapter 23

Search

SALLY OPENED her mouth to call, then closed it. It might not be a smart idea to let everyone else within earshot know what she'd heard. Not till she was absolutely sure who were friends and who were foes.

Again she listened, and now there was nothing to hear but dry leaves stirring in the wind. Which direction had the call come from? The house or the barn?

Knowing that wind could carry sound or blow it away, she wet a finger and held it up. The breeze cooled the side of her finger nearest to the barn. That settled it.

The barn was a huge shell of weather-silvered wood. When she pushed in past the sagging door and looked around, her scalp crept. Late afternoon sunlight shone through the cracks between the boards and through the ragged holes in the roof and walls, but even so it was a shadowy, secretive place. It smelled mouldy and dusty, and very faintly of cows. But it must have been decades since any animals had been kept here.

Something fluttered in a high corner, near the roof. Pigeons or swallows, Sally guessed. Or owls. Or bats. She turned around in a circle, noting the hayloft where someone might lie hidden, and the row of stalls. There wasn't much else to see except a decrepit-looking ladder lying on the floor beside the nearest wall.

A door in the opposite corner might, she thought, lead to a storage room. She decided to search that first, and started toward it. Halfway across the floor she heard an ominous crackling sound and felt the boards sagging under her feet.

Sally stopped dead. The crackling sound continued. The floor was so old and rotten, it was almost ready to collapse. Any moment now she might plunge through.

At once she dropped to her hands and knees, to spread out her weight, and crawled back up the slope of boards toward the wall. On the way she noticed something else.

Footprints. The floor was deep in gritty dust, and a lot of it had been disturbed. Some of the prints were large, some smaller. But they didn't seem to lead anywhere.

She rose from her knees and whacked clouds of dust from her jeans. Then she walked cautiously along beside the wall, where the floor seemed more solid, until she reached the corner room. It turned out to be a tiny square space lined with empty shelves. There were no footprints, no sign at all that anybody had been here in decades.

"Now for the loft," she muttered. "First, check out that ladder..." Again she froze. A voice spoke somewhere near. The sagging door creaked and hard shoes clacked across the floorboards.

"What makes you so sure she came in here?" It was Peter's voice.

"Because I saw her." Ermine sounded impatient. "I was looking out the window and she was going in this direction. Where else could she have gone?"

No use trying to hide. Sally pushed open the storeroom door and stepped out. "Hello, Ermine. Peter." She smiled at him past Ermine's shoulder, but he didn't smile back.

"I'm getting just a little bit tired of this," Ermine said evenly.

"You don't mind if I look around, do you?"

"Of course I mind! This is private property!"

"Then I guess you'd know whether Valerie Hewens was hiding

around here somewhere." Sally paused. "Or being held prisoner."

Ermine's eyes widened. Then she laughed aloud. "Valerie held prisoner! Here? What am I, the Wicked Witch of the West?"

"She's not here," Peter said huskily.

"Are you sure? I think she is."

"Oh, Sally!" Ermine was still laughing and shaking her head.

"Because," she said coolly, "I heard Valerie's voice just now. I was out in the woods. I'm sure it came from this direction."

Ermine stared. "What?"

"But that's impossible!" Peter yelped.

"Oh?" Sally turned on him. "How do you know?"

"Well — I looked. I've looked everywhere!"

"Maybe you didn't look hard enough," Sally said. "Ermine, I want to search this barn. Loft, stalls, sheds, under the floor." She swung an arm around. "Are you going to tell me I can't?"

She held Ermine's eyes. It was a challenge: there was a tug of wills between them. After a moment Ermine tossed up her hands. "Okay. If you're so sure I'm guilty, we'll do this. But we'll do it by the book. I'll call the police and have them search."

"I never said you were guilty!"

But Ermine was already on her way out, leaving Sally and Peter alone in the dim barn.

"Didn't I tell you to leave well enough alone?" he said through his teeth.

"It isn't well enough!" she flashed back. "Peter, I don't understand you. Don't you want Val to be found? Is she a threat to you in some way?"

His face bunched up with anger and frustration. Then it smoothed out, and his dark eyes smiled sadly. "I tried to warn you earlier today. You're just too mulish to listen, aren't you?"

"I call it being persistent."

"Sally, I admire you tremendously. You're brave and smart and tougher than you look. I really don't want you hurt."

"Then tell me what you know," she said urgently. "Help me get at the truth!"

He hesitated. Then his face darkened and he swung away from her. "I don't know anything."

"That is a flat-out lie!" But she had to say it to his back.

In the next twenty minutes, while they waited together, she tried a dozen times to get him to open up. But he only shrugged, shook his head and kept turning his face away. Talk about being mulish!

It was a relief when Ermine walked in followed by Detective R.J. Braun. He flashed an irritated look at Sally. "This better not be a wild goose chase."

She raised her eyebrows. "My last tip got results, didn't it?"

He grunted, then turned to Ermine. "Any other outbuildings besides this barn?"

"There are two sheds out back. Closer to the house is the garage. Oh, and tell your men to be careful of this floor, it's not safe."

"Then I guess you won't object if we rip it up to see what's underneath?"

"Go right ahead." Ermine paused, then added, "By the time you're finished, my workers will have gone home. You can search the house and studio then. Including my personal apartment. I don't want even the shadow of a doubt left in anybody's mind."

Braun studied her face a moment, then nodded. "You folks can wait at the house until we finish."

"Fine." Ermine smiled thinly at Sally and waved at the barn's crumbling door. "After you!"

Chapter 24

Not a Trace

THEY WAITED in the living room of Ermine's apartment. An hour after the search began, Braun brought one of his men to the house and they carried on there.

Nobody tried to talk. Sally sat on the sofa unobtrusively watching Ermine and Peter. Ermine sat in an easy chair idly sketching on a pad of paper, or turning the pages of a magazine. Hearing the officers' heavy footsteps as they went from room to room, her mouth tightened, but that was the only sign that she wasn't perfectly comfortable.

Under that cool surface she was steaming mad, and Sally couldn't blame her. If Valerie was hidden on the property, Ermine almost certainly didn't know about it. To her this search must seem an unforgivable invasion.

Peter hardly sat down at all. He paced, looked out the window until the deepening dusk made it impossible to see anything, then paced again. His hands, clasped behind his back, were red and white with strain. He refused to meet Sally's eyes.

When Braun suddenly appeared in the doorway of the living room, they all looked up. Sally heard a sharp indrawn breath, but she never could be sure whose it was.

"She's not here," he said bluntly.

Peter abruptly sat down on the sofa next to Sally. She saw with alarm that his face was papery white and his hands were trembling. He looked as if he was on the brink of collapse.

Ermine threw down her magazine. "Peter! Let me get you some water!" She hurried out. When she came back with a glass he waved it away.

"I'm all right. It's just..." He looked up at Braun, who was staring at him curiously. "I was hoping you'd find something, I guess."

Was he? Sally wondered. Was this the shock of disappointment — or relief?

"You found nothing at all?" she asked.

"Not a hair, not a trace. The place is clean."

"What about those footprints in the barn?"

He looked at her sourly. "All the wrong size."

"Some would be mine, some would be Peter's," Ermine said. "We were in there checking the barn's condition a few weeks ago."

"Uh-huh. Well, Miss Jones, thank you for being so patient. We'll be getting out of your hair now. I'll take the celebrated detective with me."

Sally followed him silently down the stairs and out the front door. He said nothing as they walked around the house to where she'd left Tasha's car.

Then she stopped and faced him. The parking area was well lit, so she could see just how forbidding he looked.

"Detective Braun, I'm not some airhead with a wild imagination. I did hear Valerie's voice."

"Look," he said heavily, "it's been a long day. I'm not going to argue with you. What you prob'ly heard was an owl, there's lots of them around."

"An owl in the daytime?" She gave him a knife-edged look as she took out Tasha's keys. "An owl that said 'Please help me'?"

"Sally, she isn't *here*. That's flat. Did that bump on your head shake your brain loose, or what?"

"If I could explain, I would." She thumped the car roof with her fist. "All I can think is, she ran away — or was taken away — in the half hour before you arrived."

"Let me see you get in that car," he said quietly. Sally recognized steel when she heard it. Seething, she unlocked the car, yanked open the door and climbed in.

Braun slammed the door and stepped back. "Now, let me see you drive away. And this time, stay home a while, eh? Give this poor cop a break!"

Chapter 25

Lacey on the Line

"SALLY! IT'S MOM! On the kitchen phone!"

Sally hurried out of the bathroom, pulling on a terrycloth robe and tossing her dripping hair down her back. She yelled over the banister, "I'll be right there!"

Scurrying down the stairs at just short of break-neck speed, she grabbed the phone from its cradle and dropped into a chair at the kitchen table. "Mom! When are you coming home?"

At the sound of Lacey's comfortable laughter, Sally's spirits rose. "Now, that's what a mother likes to hear. I'm sorry, Sally, but I've been asked to stay and lead a writing workshop. The original leader got sick. Three more days should do it. What have you been up to?"

"What have I been up to?" Sally took a deep breath. Then, briefly and crisply, she gave her mother a rundown of events since Saturday, three days ago. Outlining the case in this dry, factual way helped her see it more clearly. And she wasn't pleased with what she saw.

"Almost all I have are questions and guesses," she grumbled. "There are so few hard facts! Leads keep fizzling away to nothing, people won't talk — I'm tearing my hair out!"

"This doesn't sound like Lacey Sharp's daughter!" Her mother's tone was half teasing, half serious. "You're an experienced investigator, Sally, you know some cases take longer than others to pan out. Some never do. At least you've stopped Alys in her career of crime."

"Yes, but a killer is still on the loose and Valerie's still missing."

"Well... isn't it just possible that those two facts may be related?"

She frowned. "Mom, what do you mean?"

"I mean Detective Braun may have the right slant on Valerie's disappearance. The police aren't always wrong, you know. They are the professionals. And this case..." Lacey's hesitation came through clearly. "Sally, there's murder involved. This case is dangerous. I think you should drop it."

"Mom!" She sat up straight and stared in horror at the phone. "Not you too! No way, I'm not ready to give up yet!"

Her mother seemed to be holding her breath. Then she let it out in a sigh. "Oh, Sally. You're too old for me to tell you what to do. Just... be careful. And if real danger threatens, back off. Will you promise me that?"

"All right, Mom. I promise."

"Love you, sweetheart."

Sally was smiling as she hung up the phone and went upstairs to towel-dry her hair. A talk with her mother never failed to brace her up when she was feeling down and defeated. Even now, when her mom was trying to talk her out of pursuing the case. She always felt stronger, knowing she had her mom at her back.

"No, I'm not quitting yet," she said aloud, as she picked up her cellphone and tapped in Tasha's number. "The facts are out there, I just have to dig for them. And there's still one more lead I haven't followed up."

Impatiently she listened to the ringtone at the other end.

"Hello?"

"Tasha! Are you up for a trip to Toronto?"

Chapter 26

Road Trip

"WHAT A GREAT day to be on the road!" Tasha squinted against the sunshine that slanted in through the windows of the red Honda.

"Too bad Fay couldn't come with us." Sally gazed thoughtfully out at the mellow late-summer landscape rolling by on both sides of the highway. Fay had gone to work at Jones & Hewens that morning.

"Maybe it's just as well." Tasha wrinkled her nose. "She's so hung up on the idea that Peter's totally innocent, she'd be on our case the whole time."

"But we're not out to prove he's guilty. We're just trying to find out what he's hiding."

"Try telling Fay that!"

The drive to Toronto hadn't started well. Dylan had tailed Sally almost from her front door, and she'd had to call on all her driving skills to shake him off.

Tasha couldn't believe it. "You'd think he had better things to do than follow us around!"

They finally lost him by ducking down an exit ramp at the last moment. The white Corvette shot past on an inner lane.

Tasha laughed and sat back. "What a pain in the butt! What's the big idea?"

"I think the idea is to teach Miss Upstart Snoop a lesson." Sally blew out an exasperated breath. "But don't laugh, Tash. You're a target too. We got the better of him once or twice and his overgrown ego can't take it."

"And Alys would be egging him on." Tasha narrowed her eyes. "Don't underestimate him. He could be dangerous. Remember that knife?"

"You just bet I do!"

After that they stayed on secondary roads for a while, ate lunch at a little hamburger diner, rejoined the highway farther on and drove into Toronto early in the afternoon.

THE SCHOOL of Fashion Arts was a long white-and-black ceramic tile building that looked more like a bowling alley than a college. Sally had been thinking of different ways to get at the information she hoped to find. As they drove along the street in front of the building looking for a parking spot, she broke into a smile.

"Look, they've made it easy for us!"

A banner was draped above the entrance. OPEN HOUSE & EX-HIBITION – ALL WELCOME

They left the Honda in a parking lot behind the building and found their way to a glass-walled front lobby. Students in eye-catching outfits handed out programs to a stream of visitors.

"Fashion show at three o'clock in the auditorium! Don't miss it!" A girl in a mini-dress sparkling with tiny LED lights and a matching velvet hat handed Tasha a program.

Tasha's eyes widened as she looked her up and down. "Did you design your own clothes? Wild!"

The girl laughed. "If you think this is wild, go take a look at the 'Most Outrageous' exhibit."

"That we've got to see!"

"What about former students?" Sally asked. "Is any of their work on display?"

"Check out the Retrospective Rooms. Top floor."

Tasha insisted they see the "Most Outrageous" exhibit first. It lived up to its billing.

"Can you imagine wearing this?" Sally stared at a coat made of aluminum can pull-tabs and rubber bands.

Tasha grinned. "No, but I can see Alys in it. It's definitely her!"

They strolled on along the corridors, in and out of theme rooms. "It really is a shame Fay had to miss this," Tasha said. "You know how she feels about clothes. She'd be in heaven!"

On the top floor they found several rooms labelled with the names of decades. Music typical of each era floated from the doorways as they walked by. It was quieter up here, with only a handful of people wandering from room to room.

"Here we are," Sally said. "The Nineties." They walked in.

"I'll bet this is a fitting room normally." Tasha pointed at a cluster of dress forms standing together in a corner like gossiping neighbours. "You can see why they call them Judys."

Long work tables had been pushed back along the walls. Examples of student work were arranged to show the fashion design process from first sketch through to the finished outfit. Most of the designs looked dated after so many years, but a few had kept their freshness.

"Look at this!" Sally pointed at a sketch of a floor-length ball gown made of trailing peacock feathers. "Feathers on silk base," she read, peering closer. "Isn't that stunning?"

"It wouldn't last more than one evening," Tasha said with a shrug.

"Yeah, but what an evening!" Sally's eyes shone.

Tasha chuckled. "Get your feet back on the ground, Sal! Dresses like that cost a fortune. I'll bet this student is a famous designer now."

"I bet you're right. Where's the signature?"

"Um..." Tasha squinted. "Can't read it. What a scrawl!"

"Yes," said a pleasant new voice behind them. "That was her all over. No discipline!"

Chapter 27

Flash From the Past

THEY TURNED around to see a smiling silver-haired woman of about sixty. She wore a jacket and matching skirt cut from a rich East Indian print fabric, set off with silver and amethyst jewellery.

"Let me guess," Sally said. "You're a grad."

"One of the first. Melba Capra." She held out a hand. "I'm also an instructor. Are you girls thinking of coming to TSFA?"

"Well, no." Sally named herself and Tasha as she returned the warm handshake. "But we know two of your former students. In fact, we've worked for them. Peter Hewens and Ermine Jones. Do you remember them?"

"Do I!" Ms. Capra's smile widened. "Peter is rather unforgettable, don't you think? I'm sure most of his female classmates thought so. Those looks won't do him any harm at all in the fashion business. Of course he has talent, too. But you said you work for him?"

"As models, part time," Tasha put in. "He and Ermine have their own label now — Corduroy Rose."

"Good for them!" She beamed. "Not many do so well. The fashion industry is hip-deep in failed ventures. But Ermine was always so hard-working and ambitious, she was bound to succeed."

She turned and walked to the wall nearest the door. It was a solid mass of photographs, big and small. "Let's see... yes, here we are."

Ms. Capra's finger came to rest on a photograph of two girls sitting together on a set of concrete steps: the school steps, Sally guessed. One was a younger, happier-looking Ermine. The other was a plump blond with a lazy grin.

"The Siamese Twins, they called themselves. Which was funny, because they were totally different. Ermine so intense and energetic, Kendra so laid back."

"Kendra?"

"Kendra Molson. That was her maiden name, of course."

Sally felt shaken as she gazed at the blond girl's face, once so alive. It was like looking at a ghost.

Melba Capra tapped the picture again. "Now, that girl really disappointed me."

"Kendra? Not up to standard, huh?" Tasha asked.

Ms. Capra looked startled. "Up to standard? Kendra was my star pupil! In spite of being such a pain in the neck. She had a real gift, Kendra did."

"Really?" Sally was surprised. Somehow her interview with Ermine had left her thinking Kendra had been short on talent.

"Really! And what does she do? Drops out and gets married to a rich man from her old home town. I was furious!"

"Why was she such a pain in the neck?"

"She never lived up to her potential." Ms. Capra half smiled, half frowned. "Lazy. Not good at listening. Unwilling to do the necessary work to develop her designs into something wearable. You'd almost think she didn't value her own work."

"That drawing we were looking at..." Sally crossed to the table again and looked at the sketch of the peacock-feather gown. It was beautiful, but something about it made her feel slightly queasy. She couldn't pinpoint the cause, yet she couldn't shake it off.

"You're right, that was one of hers. She loved evening wear and she had a flair for it. If only... Oh, well." Ms. Capra flung up her hands. "It was her choice. No doubt she's perfectly happy as a queen bee somewhere out in the boondocks."

"Then you don't know—" Tasha broke off as Sally poked her in the ribs.

"Know what?" The teacher looked bewildered. "Did something happen to Kendra?"

Sally hesitated, then quietly told her of Kendra Mahon's death.

"Killed in a burglary! How terrible!" Ms. Capra's hands flew to her face. She stood a moment lost in memory, then dropped her hands.

"I'm sure I kept some of her best sketches," she murmured, half to herself. "I'd like to dig them out and display some of them as a sort of memorial. If only I had time..."

"We'd love to do the digging for you," Sally said gently. "Kendra was a Knollvale girl, and that's where we're from."

"Would you? I really ought to keep circulating. Oh, and..." She gave them an apologetic smile. "Sorry about that 'boondocks' remark."

Melba Capra's office was a large, grey-carpeted room on the same floor. On one wall was a collage of fashion photos and drawings above a bank of filing cabinets. She slid open a drawer and after some searching pulled out two manila folders and handed them to Sally. Then she hurried out, promising to be back in half an hour.

Sally and Tasha pulled up chairs, one on each side of the desk, and opened the files. Tasha started flipping through sketch after sketch. "What are we looking for?"

"I'm not sure." Sally's forehead creased. "I have a strange feeling about Kendra's work. Sleuth's instinct, maybe. It reminds me of something, but I can't think what."

"Some of these are fabulous." Tasha whistled admiringly. "To think they were never turned into real clothes! And now they never will be. Nobody will ever wear them. What a shame."

Sally was silent. Tasha looked up and saw her staring down at a sheet of paper that lay on the desk between her hands. She looked shaken.

"Sal? Found something?"

She glanced up, then back down at the paper, and nodded slowly. "I think so, Tash."

"Well?" Tasha craned her neck to see. "What?"

"I think... I'm looking at a motive for murder."

Chapter 28

Like a Bad Penny

"ARE YOU PLANNING to explain that remark?" Tasha put on an exaggerated air of patience. "Or are you going to leave me to die of curiosity?"

Sally bit her lip, thought a moment, then shook her head. "Humour me, okay? I've seen so many leads in this case turn into dead ends. I want to dig a little more, before I shoot my mouth off again."

They went through both files carefully. Sally chose the twelve best sketches and spread them out on the desk. She set two others on the filing cabinet.

When Melba Capra returned, she looked over the twelve sketches and smiled approvingly at Sally. "You have a good eye. Sure you won't reconsider and join us after all?"

Sally laughed. "Thanks, but I already have a career mapped out." Deliberately she added, "I'm planning to become a private investigator. A detective."

"A detective!" For a moment Ms. Capra looked stunned. Then her eyes flickered as an idea struck her. "This is about Kendra, isn't it? You're investigating her death?"

"No, the police are doing that. But her death may have a bearing on my case. And I think you may have steered me in the right direction."

Sally watched her uncertainly. She could never tell how people, especially older people, would react on being told that this seventeen-year-old high school girl was a detective on a case. Some laughed at her, some thought she was cute, some became hostile.

Melba Capra didn't react in any of those ways. After reflecting for a minute she said, "If I've helped at all, I'm glad. I hope the police catch whoever killed Kendra and lock him up for good!"

Sally relaxed. "There's one more way you can help. Let me borrow these for a while." She picked up the two sketches from the file cabinet. "I promise I'll return them when I'm through."

"That's fine," Ms. Capra said quietly. "And please let me know how it all turns out."

SALLY AND TASHA stayed to see the fashion show. They felt they owed it to Fay, who would want to know every exquisite detail.

Then they headed back, stopping for a quick bite of supper on the way. "I'll drop you off at home," Sally said as they neared the outskirts of Knollvale. "Then I have to make a call."

"What about?" Tasha folded her arms stubbornly across her seatbelt. "I know you've got something bubbling in that head of yours, Sally. Don't think you're going to shut me out!"

"It's nothing exciting, I swear! I just want to set up an interview with someone in Kendra's home."

The somebody Sally reached was Kendra Mahon's housekeeper. At first she would hardly say a word, but Peter Hewens' name worked on her like a charm. She became eager to talk.

"Honestly, he was like a bad penny, always turning up. She gave him a key of his own — can you believe it? Mr. Mahon really got ticked off, let me tell you!"

Sally put a smile in her voice. "I'll bet you could tell some interesting stories, couldn't you?"

"Oh, you bet I could! That is, if somebody made it worth my while," the woman added in a suggestive tone. "Which newspaper did you say you worked for?"

Sally hadn't mentioned a newspaper at all. "Why don't we talk this over in person?" She hoped she wasn't betraying her dislike of the woman's money-grubbing approach. "I'd love a chance to see the house, too. Say, an hour from now? Thanks!"

FAY AND TASHA were both at the Dolinski house, sitting in front of the television with a big bowl of popcorn between them, when Sally dropped in late that evening.

"What a day it's been!" She wilted onto the sofa next to Tasha. "I could fall asleep right here!"

"Not till you bring us up to speed on the case." Tasha went and got her a glass of cold ginger ale, and moved the bowl of popcorn closer. "My parents and my two brothers are out at some kids' movie, so go ahead and talk."

"I'm ready to lay it all out for you now." Sally sat up and stretched wearily. "Because I'll need your help tomorrow, both of you. And, Fay, please wait until I'm finished before you bite my head off, okay?"

She took a sip of soda and started talking. When she'd finished, Tasha looked excited and Fay was upset. "It's so hard to believe," she muttered.

"I know," Sally said with a sigh. "I wish I were totally wrong. But I know I'm on the right track!"

"How are you going to get him to meet you?" Tasha asked.

"Why don't I try now? I think I know what'll hook him." Sally pulled out her phone and keyed in Peter's number. He answered on the fifth ring.

"Peter? Sally Sharp here."

A silence followed. Then, "What now?"

She went at him head-on. "I want you to meet me. I've found out something important."

"What on earth would that be?" he demanded.

"It's about Valerie." He tried to interrupt but she talked on. "Meet me tomorrow at Rattlesnake Point lookout. Ten a.m. sharp. Don't be late!"

She clicked off. Then looked up to find Tasha and Fay gazing at her, all eyebrows up.

"What are the odds he won't be there?" Fay said.

"I know. But it's worth the gamble."

"Could be risky," Tasha said with a frown.

"I know that too. Stop worrying!"

Chapter 29

Danger at Rattlesnake Point

SALLY WAS GLAD she'd worn a denim jacket over her T-shirt. The last time she'd been here at Rattlesnake Point, she'd broiled under the hot sun. Today the sky was heavy with iron-grey clouds, and there was a hint of fall in the brisk wind. The stone retaining wall felt cold through the seat of her jeans, so she got up and walked back and forth.

A glance over the wall showed her the tops of two heads, one glossy black and one curly red-brown. Fay and Tasha were sitting directly below, between the wall and a row of scrubby cedars. If they didn't stand up and if Peter didn't walk too close to the edge of the lookout, and if nobody sneezed, he would never know they were there.

And that, Sally thought, was a lot of ifs.

She pulled out her phone to check the time. "It's ten o'clock. Where is he?"

"If he's not here by ten-thirty," Tasha said, "I vote we go for coffee. This is boring!"

"And there are spiders, ugh!" Fay said.

"Well, he — Wait, here he comes."

The sound of a motor suddenly grew louder as a car rounded the base of the cliff below the lookout and roared up the twisting road. Sally's brows drew together. Wasn't Peter's car yellow? This was white. And... she groaned. Yes, it was a Corvette.

"It's Dylan again! He'll ruin everything!"

"Then we'd better come out." Tasha was climbing over the wall as she spoke. Fay followed more slowly, looking nervous.

The Corvette screeched to a stop in the gravelled parking area of the lookout, raising a cloud of dust. Dylan got out and leaned on the open door. "Thought I saw you heading this way, Sally Sharp." His smirk was more irritating than usual.

"I think Eddie's getting tired of this game." Sally nodded at the driver. From what she could see of his expression, he wasn't happy.

Tasha waved at him. He pretended he hadn't seen her. She laughed. "Yeah, I bet right now he wishes he'd stuck to hopscotch."

"Eddie," Dylan said in a casual voice, "get out and open the back door. No, just one, the one on this side." Eddie did that, meanwhile carefully not looking any of the girls in the face. Then he slid back behind the wheel.

Dylan showed his teeth. "See? Eddie does what he's told. You girls could take lessons from him."

At any other time Sally would have enjoyed telling Dylan off in a way he wouldn't soon forget. Right this minute, he was simply a nuisance. How was she going to get rid of him before Peter got here?

"Look, I'd be glad to talk about whatever's bothering you. But not here and now. How about—"

"How about you shut up and get in the car?"

Sally bit off a sharp answer. Dylan had raised his right hand above the car door and let her see what he was holding. Not a knife this time. A gun. A deadly looking semi-automatic pistol. Pointing straight at her stomach.

All her muscles tightened up and so did her voice. "This is a big, big mistake, Dylan."

"Yeah. Yours." He stepped away from the Corvette and stalked toward her. She took a step back and heard Fay and Tasha move.

She was ready for him to jump her. *Just let him get close enough, and I might — might! — have a chance of disarming him.*

But when he jumped, it wasn't at her. In a split second he had Fay in a one-armed headlock, with the muzzle of the gun pressing into her right temple. Her scream choked off as he pulled his arm tight across her throat.

Sally stood absolutely still. Tasha hissed in horror. Dylan's smile widened.

"That's right. You just be good little girls, or this one gets it first. And you'll be next, Sally."

Play for time. The right moment will come. "What..." She swallowed and cleared her clogged throat. "What do you want?"

"Well now, that's something I'll have to think about. It'll have to be good, to pay you back what I owe you. Meantime..." His gloating voice went cold. "The three of you, get in the car. Back seat. Now!"

Sally moved jerkily, her muscles stiff with tension. She willed herself to relax. She had to be ready to move fast when the right moment came. Dylan stepped back, dragging Fay with him, and jerked his head at the Corvette. Sally and Tasha walked slowly toward the open back door.

She guessed later that they'd all been so riveted on what was happening that they simply hadn't noticed the sound of the other car as it approached. When it drove into the parking area, it seemed to burst out of nowhere.

It was the moment Sally had been waiting for. Dylan's attention jerked aside and his gun hand swerved. She was near enough. With a lunge she grabbed the barrel of the gun and twisted it upward and to the right, twisting his wrist with it.

"Tash, Fay!" she yelled. "Run!"

Chapter 30

Tackling Peter

FAY BROKE FREE. But by now Sally had lost the advantage of surprise, and Dylan's muscular strength was starting to count.

Next moment he lurched, yelled and went spinning across the parking lot. He landed heavily and lay stunned, then rolled over with a groan. Sally stood panting. "What?" she gasped. Whatever had just happened, she hadn't done it.

Then she became aware of someone at standing at her shoulder. She whipped around. "Peter!"

Peter stood with his fists clenched, his eyes narrowed at Dylan. Tasha cheered and grabbed Fay in a hug. At the same moment an engine revved and the Corvette took off with a spray of gravel, the back door still swinging open. Dylan scrambled to his feet and frantically searched the ground around him.

"Where's the gun?" Sally asked Peter, after a final gasp.

"I've got it." He took it out of his pocket and flicked on the safety catch. Then he dropped it back in and calmly settled the fit of his tweed jacket. They all looked at Dylan.

"Hey, listen." He laughed nervously. "It was a joke. You girls got the wrong idea!"

"No," Sally said. "I think we understood you pretty well. I think the police will, too."

"I didn't hurt you. You can't prove a thing, so don't try." He started away, then turned back. Sally felt cold when she saw the look of hatred in his eyes. "You'll get what's coming to you, Sally Sharp.

You will. Just wait."

Tasha laughed scornfully. "Hey, take it easy on Eddie when you catch him," she yelled after him as he tramped away down the road. "I kinda like him."

"Fay, are you all right?" Sally asked anxiously.

"Yes — thanks to Peter." She grabbed his hand and looked up at him with shining eyes. He smiled down at her, embarrassed.

"I was glad to help. But I don't understand why you're all here. Didn't you say you wanted to see me alone, Sally?"

"Uh... yes." This was going to be ten times harder because of what they'd just been through. If Peter hadn't arrived just then... It was possible they owed him their lives.

"Oh, go ahead and tell him what you found out." Fay was smiling. "I'm sure he can explain. In my book, he's a hero."

Sally sighed. "All right." She went over to the Honda and got the manila folder she'd left on the back seat. Then she walked back to Peter and flipped open the folder.

"Can you explain this?"

His face tightened. "Where did you get it?"

"Never mind. You recognize it?" It was a sketch of a two-piece outfit, the skirt slit to streamers and the coat cut long and narrow. On the lapel was a fabric rose in the same colour as the jacket.

"Looks like an outfit from Jones & Hewens's spring season, doesn't it?" she persisted. "We saw it in the studio, right?"

"It isn't... exactly... the same."

That sinking feeling settled again in her stomach. "Not exactly. But almost. Look at the signature, Peter."

He looked, but said nothing. Sally went on, "It says Kendra Molson, doesn't it? And there's the date. Fourteen years ago."

The wind fluttered the sketch. She closed the folder. "Here's

110

what happened," she said evenly. "Kendra had copies of some of her student sketches in her home. Her best ones, probably. I can see how she'd want to keep them, even if she threw away everything else from her student days. You were her protégé; you were in her house all the time. You found her old sketches. You copied them and passed them off as your own. Maybe you thought she'd never notice."

She took a deep breath. "But then she found out, didn't she? And threatened to make a stink that would have smashed your career to bits. And you lost your cool and hit her. Maybe you didn't mean to kill her. But she's dead."

She watched his face. Right up to the last moment she hoped he would say something to prove her wrong.

But he hadn't said anything, and he hadn't looked at her. Now he switched his eyes to her and, unexpectedly, smiled. "I really wish you'd stayed out of this!"

"Peter—"

"Yes, Sally, you've got the answer."

"No!" Fay cried. "I don't believe it!"

Sally touched Fay's arm. "I wish it wasn't true. Believe me, I do." She held Peter's eyes. He still smiled, but he looked trapped. She swallowed a lump in her throat and plowed on.

"The Mahons' housekeeper will swear that he had his own key to the house. He was 'always turning up,' she says. Kendra kept the best of her old student sketches in a carton in the attic: I've been up there and I've seen them. Maybe Peter got the impression that she didn't care about them. So, he... borrowed them."

"But, Sally." Tasha furrowed her forehead. "Those sketches were over a dozen years old. How could he hope to pass them off as new? Wouldn't the designs look dated?"

Peter gave them a thin smile. "The retro look's in style, haven't you noticed? Besides," he added, "Kendra's work was too brilliant to ever look dated."

"But she did care about those old designs, didn't she?" Sally persisted. "She hadn't forgotten. So, when did she find out?"

"It was at the showing in the Lightstone house. Kendra wasn't on the guest list, but she turned up at the last minute and of course Mrs. Lightstone wouldn't turn her away: they belonged to the same social set. I found out later that Kendra was already suspicious — she must have heard rumours. When she viewed the outfits, she recognized some of them as near-copies of her designs."

"And that same evening she died."

"Yes." He stared down at his hands. His face looked grey. Sally wondered if he was recalling that last angry meeting with Kendra.

"What did she say to you, Peter? What made you lose it?"

Sally realized that she was still looking for ways to excuse him. But there was no way out of this. Peter was a murderer.

"You're good, Sally." He gave himself a shake, as if shrugging a weight off his shoulders. "I was hoping you were bluffing, but you really are on the right track. And now, I suppose, you'll go to the police with what you know?"

"Can you give me one reason why I shouldn't?"

They faced each other. His dark eyes gleamed with anger, and for a moment he looked dangerous. Sally tensed, remembering he had Dylan's gun in his pocket. She felt Fay and Tasha close in on either side of her.

Then his face softened in a smile. "Yes, I can. It's this: I didn't kill Kendra. I didn't steal her designs, either."

"So, who—"

"Ermine."

112

Chapter 31
Who, How, When, Why

THERE WAS a stunned silence, then Fay gasped. "Ermine! Of course! Why didn't we see that before?"

"Because Peter claimed the designs were his," Sally snapped. He hadn't talked his way out of this yet.

"I didn't want to. But I thought they were Ermine's designs, at least at first. And she told me it would be good public relations if I was named as the designer." He flushed slightly. "She said I had the looks to fit the image. It was all media hype."

"Where did Ermine get the designs?" Sally asked.

"She'd had them for years. Since when they were students rooming together, in fact. She said Kendra gave them to her when she dropped out; asked her to dispose of them. I never heard anything about any box in Kendra's attic."

Sally thought about that. One way and another, he was starting to convince her. She looked around at the ring of faces: Tasha's thoughtful, Peter's drawn with strain, Fay's bright and smiling.

The wind tugged at her jacket and she shivered. "Why don't we go get some hot coffee?"

THEY FOUND a cozy-looking coffee shop in a small town a mile south of Rattlesnake Point. Fay managed to end up squeezed into one side of the booth at Peter's side.

Sally sat beside Tasha across the faux marble tabletop from Peter. She watched his face carefully as he talked.

113

"You nailed the motive, Sally. I suspected after a while that the designs weren't really Ermine's. For one thing, she would never let me see any preliminary sketches. And what I'd seen of her other work hadn't impressed me that much. I couldn't figure out how she was suddenly coming up with these dynamite designs."

"When did you know for sure?" Fay prompted.

"It was about two weeks after Kendra was killed." His mouth tightened. "Ermine had left her appointment book in her apartment and I went to get it for her, since she was busy with a buyer. The drawings were out on top of her desk. I guess she'd forgotten to lock them away. There were about two dozen of them, and they were all signed Kendra Molson. Kendra had a very distinctive — messy — signature." He smiled. "You had to know how to read it."

"How did Ermine change the signature?" Tasha asked.

"She didn't. Just copied the drawings — she had enough skill for that — and added her own name."

Sally's eyebrows went up. "She actually told you this?"

"Well, she couldn't very well deny it, could she? The evidence was right under my nose." He looked grim. "Then I asked her if Kendra'd found out, and if that was why she died."

"And?" Sally's hands tightened around her mug.

"She denied it absolutely." He sipped at his coffee. "Said she knew nothing about it. I didn't know whether to believe her or not, until I overheard something she said to Alys."

"So Alys knew something, did she?" Tasha put in. "We figured she did. Was she blackmailing Ermine?"

Peter set down his mug. "Yes, that's the impression I got. I didn't hear it all, but Alys was hinting about needing more money... 'or I might just decide to tell the cops what happened to Mrs. Mahon,' she said."

Fay made a noise of disgust. "What a weasel!"

"They both shut up as soon as they saw me, of course."

"So, why didn't you go to the police?" Tasha demanded.

"That's what I should have done, right then. If I had, I wouldn't be in this spot now, and Valerie..." He cut that off with a shake of his head. "I thought I had to give Ermine a chance to explain. She was my partner, I owed her that much. Can you understand?"

"I can!" Fay piped up. Peter gave her a lopsided smile.

"So that evening," he went on, "I laid it all out for her — just the way you did for me, Sally." He flicked an edgier smile at her. "She didn't deny it. Didn't say she was sorry, either. Just said things would have turned out better if Kendra had been 'more flexible.' Seems that when Kendra tackled her on it, Ermine offered her a percentage of the profits if she gave up any claim to the designs and kept her mouth shut. Kendra refused. Said she might have agreed if she'd been asked, but she hadn't been asked — and Ermine was a thief and a plagiarist. And she, Kendra, was taking the story to the media."

"Ermine must have felt totally cornered," Sally said thoughtfully. "So that's what led to the murder..."

"How is it that you discovered the body?" Tasha asked.

"Simple enough. Ermine said she'd heard Kendra was there, and would I please go find her and invite her to have coffee with us after the showing? So I went looking... The perfect fall guy." His mouth twisted. "Later, when I confronted her, she took it so quietly that I thought she felt beaten. She asked for a few days' grace to put her affairs in order. Of course I said yes. I thought she meant she was going to turn herself in."

"That was a tad naive," Sally said dryly.

"I can see that now. Then, it seemed reasonable. The following Saturday I was in Toronto on errands, and when I got back that night, and saw the cop cars out front... Well, you know."

"Val was gone." Sally stared at him. Could all this be true? "So you're saying Ermine kidnapped her? How? And why?"

"I don't know how." He pushed his mug aside and knotted his shaking hands together. "It wasn't until the next day that I found out Ermine did it. Well," he said to Sally with a half smile, "you remember how I begged you to take the case, that first evening."

She nodded. "How did she break the news?"

"She was very businesslike. Even pleasant. Soon as I came to the studio on the next day, she called me into her office and offered me a cup of coffee. Then she said, 'You can stop worrying about Val. I've got her.' Just like that."

Tasha whistled softly. Peter ducked his head. "Yeah. It just about knocked me flat. It took me a moment to understand what she meant."

"But," Sally said thoughtfully, "she wouldn't tell you where she was holding Val."

"That's right. She just said Val was safe. Not hurt. But I — I didn't know what to believe. All I could think was, she — Ermine — must've been the one that clubbed old Mrs. Engstrom over the head, too. So she wasn't squeamish."

"And you still didn't go to the police?"

He took a long breath and let it out slowly. "You've got to understand. She said that if I told the police, or anyone, about what I knew or suspected, then she couldn't risk letting Val go. And I would never see my sister again."

116

Chapter 32

The Impossible Witness

"DO YOU SEE now, Sally? That's why I kept telling you to cancel the investigation."

"I thought you were threatening me!"

"I knew how it sounded and I hoped you'd take it to heart. Not just for Val's sake. For yours too, Sally. Ermine is capable of anything."

"Maybe she's paying Dylan to harass you," Fay suggested.

Sally laughed shortly. "I don't think he needs to be paid for that." She looked at Peter. "So you just carried on as usual? Was that one of Ermine's demands?"

He nodded. "She said everything about Jones & Hewens had to look normal, until she was ready."

"Ready for what?"

"She wouldn't tell me. Just that it would take her a few days. I think she means to get out of the country. She promised that she would tell me where to find Val, safe and sound, as soon as she was safe herself. She also said, cool as anything," he added grimly, "that if anything happened to her, then Val would not live long."

"One more question." Sally held his eyes. "When Braun was searching Ermine's property, you were on edge. When nothing turned up, I thought you seemed relieved. Why?"

He blinked at her, then frowned, thinking back. "Yes, I can see how suspicious that must have looked. I was torn in half. One part of me was hoping she'd be found. The other half was afraid Ermine would feel so threatened, she'd simply kill Valerie and disappear."

He rubbed a hand over his face. "This last week has been hell."

They sat in silence for a minute with their half-full mugs of coffee cooling in front of them. A passing waitress gave them a curious look. Sally turned everything over in her mind.

Peter shifted nervously. "Don't you believe me?"

Fay's hand closed protectively over his. "Of course we do!"

"Well, it all sounds fairly convincing to me." Tasha turned her palms up. "But it's Sal's case, so what we do now has to be her decision."

Peter gazed at Sally. "And?"

A reluctant smile crept over her face. "I guess that explains why there weren't any marks in the dust."

"Dust?" Peter stared at her as if she'd lost her mind. She couldn't help laughing.

"The dust on that carton of sketches in Kendra's attic. I thought you'd just been very, very careful to not leave finger marks."

"I never knew the carton was there!"

"Yes, I believe you now." She laughed again as a dazzling smile spread over his face.

Then she sobered. "What makes it all hang together is what Melba Capra said about you and Ermine. She described you as talented, but when she talked about Ermine, she only mentioned her hard work and ambition."

"That was one point I was going to make," Peter said dryly. "I might not be a match for Kendra, but I've got enough on the ball to win my own fame and fortune. I don't need to steal anybody else's work."

"Whereas Ermine is ambitious and determined, but she doesn't have that special spark. She must have reached the point where she knew she'd never be a big name. And she couldn't accept it."

"So she had to ride on somebody else's wings," Fay put in. "You know, I almost feel sorry for her."

"Don't," Peter said flatly.

Sally nodded. "Or save it until she's on trial for murder." She found a quarter in her bag and left it by her mug for a tip. "Well, Peter? Ready?" She slid to the end of the bench.

He hesitated. "For what?"

"To come down to the police station with me and tell all this to Detective Braun." She grinned. "I can't wait to see his face!"

"No."

Sally was half out of her seat. "No, what?"

"No, I can't make a statement."

She stared at him and slowly sank back down.

"What?" Tasha demanded.

Fay looked bewildered. "Why?"

"Because of Val, of course. Didn't you hear what I've been saying?"

"It's natural you'd feel that way." Sally searched for arguments that would change his mind. "But if Ermine can be convinced that the game is up—"

"How?" he demanded in a fierce whisper. "What real, hard evidence do we have that will nail her?"

"Well, the drawings..." Sally grimaced. "You're right. She's probably burnt them by now."

"But we've got the two in the folder!" Fay objected.

"She could say she never saw those, and she doesn't recall any drawings from twenty years ago. She'd say if anybody copied the drawings, it had to be her designer." Peter's smile was wry. "You see? All she has to do is deny everything. And if anyone gets arrested, it'll be me."

"Suppose we get Alys to tell what she knows?"

"And just how likely is it that Alys will cut off a nice source of funds by fingering Ermine?"

"Besides," Tasha put in, "why would Alys do us any favours?"

Peter nodded dismally. "The only thing that will nail Ermine — the only way I can speak out — is if Val's found. And that will never happen unless Ermine talks."

"Which means..." Sally closed her eyes in frustration. She felt they were running around in circles.

"It means Val is Ermine's insurance policy. Her hostage. She won't be set free until Ermine's gotten away safe and sound." He thumped his fists on the table. "Don't you see? If I get that woman arrested and jailed, I'll be condemning my sister to death!"

Chapter 33

To Find the Key

"WE'RE BACK to square one, then." Sally slid out of the booth and walked to the front of the coffee shop to pay her bill.

On the windswept pavement outside, in full daylight, she could see how haggard Peter looked. For a moment she forgot her own frustrations. The strain he'd been under since Valerie had vanished must be unbearable.

He met her eyes. "I know what you're thinking. That I'm a selfish coward. I'm willing to sit back and let a murderer go free."

"Not exactly," she said gently.

"Well, I am. What do I care if Ermine gets the justice she deserves, if it means Valerie dies?"

"I was really thinking, suppose Ermine just skips the country and you never get another word out of her?"

"I have to believe she'll send me a message as soon as she feels safe. I have to believe she's not a cold-blooded killer. If I didn't believe that, I'd have nothing to hold onto at all."

"What will you do now?" Fay asked.

"Right now? Get back to the studio. I don't want Ermine to get suspicious. You should be there too, shouldn't you?"

She smoothed back a strand of windblown hair and flashed a dimple. "Do I hear the offer of a lift?"

"You sure do." He turned toward the yellow Mustang and Fay swung gaily along beside him.

"Look at that." Tasha stifled a laugh. "She's practically skipping!"

"Uh... Fay," Sally called. "We need to talk. I'll give you a lift."

Fay looked back and mouthed, *Not now.* Sally grinned. *Now!* she mouthed back. Fay heaved a heavy sigh, thanked Peter prettily and headed back, grumbling under her breath.

"What a wet blanket you are!" she complained, as she climbed into the back seat of the Honda.

"There'll be other chances to flirt with him, don't worry." Tasha slid into the front passenger seat. "Well, Sal, what now? Seems to me we're stuck."

"Not exactly. Think: we know everything about this case now. We know who, how, when and why."

"But not where," Tasha put in.

"You got it. We know everything except where Val's being held. Unless we find her, we can't go to the police with what we know."

"She's like a key," Fay said.

"Right. So how do we find that key?" Sally was thinking aloud. "The farm property's been searched."

"Maybe Ermine has some other property?" Tasha suggested. "How would we find out?"

"Tax assessment rolls," Fay said promptly. "I could go and search them, except I'm supposed to be at Jones & Hewens. And I'm already an hour late."

"Yes, and we need you there." Sally keyed the ignition and the Honda rolled out of the parking lot and onto the highway. Over her shoulder she said, "I want you to keep an eye on Ermine and let me know when it's safe for me to search her apartment. There's still a chance she hasn't got rid of those drawings, and they're vital as evidence."

"But if we don't find Val," Fay began.

"I know. We can't risk her life. So I'll search those tax assessment rolls this afternoon."

"That's something I can do," Tasha said. "And then I think we should plan to watch Ermine — around the clock, if need be. See where she goes. She'd have to visit Val some time, wouldn't she? I mean, it's been five days since the kid vanished. She'd need food and water, at least."

"Unless—" Sally bit it off and kept her eyes on the highway as it unrolled toward her. A cold silence filled the car.

"Unless she's already dead, you mean?" Fay said in a small voice. "Would Ermine do that?"

Sally pressed her lips together. "Remember old Mrs. Engstrom? And Kendra Mahon?"

A few minutes later, Sally stopped to let Fay out at the end of the driveway to the farmhouse. She sat looking after her, remembering the time she'd imagined hearing Valerie's voice in the woods. It had to be imagination, of course. There was no other possible explanation. The police search would have caught even a mouse out of place.

There was only one problem with that. Sally wasn't in the habit of letting imagination carry her away.

Tasha nudged her arm. "What's eating you, Sal?"

Sally gave herself a shake and started the car. "Nothing I can put in words. I have this weird feeling that I know something — but I don't know what it is that I know!"

Chapter 34

Bird's-Eye View

AFTER DROPPING OFF Tasha at home to get her own car, Sally drove to police headquarters to give up Dylan's pistol. Peter had handed it over after they'd left the coffee shop, and she'd stashed it in her glove compartment.

The officer who took Sally's report pursed her lips. "That Thatcher boy is getting to be a real pain in the neck. It's going to mean more than just a talking-to, this time."

And about time, Sally thought as she left the building. She looked around for the white Corvette, but it was nowhere in sight, for once. Maybe Dylan had finally realized that he'd gone too far. Maybe he'd back off now and leave her alone. Maybe!

That sense of *almost* knowing something — something vital — was still bothering her. Sally frowned as she stood on the sidewalk outside the station. When a feeling nagged at her that strongly, she knew it wasn't imagination, but something quite different. It was instinct. The sleuthing instinct that comes from experience.

But the mysterious something stayed out of reach. She shook her head and walked along the street to where she'd left the Honda parked. A display in a shop window caught her eye. She stared.

The window belonged to a real estate office. Small pictures of houses for sale were arranged around the edges of a huge, highly detailed map of Knollvale, with coloured strings leading from the featured houses to their locations on the map.

When Sally looked closer, she saw the map was actually a photograph taken from a satellite. The detail it showed was amazing. You could pick out individual trees, cars and buildings.

That nagging hunch suddenly blossomed into an idea. She pulled out her cellphone, called City Hall and asked to be put through to the office in charge of surveys. A man's pleasant voice answered.

"Can you tell me if there was ever a complete survey done of Knollvale?" Sally asked. "An aerial survey, I mean."

"Of the city proper? There've been several."

"I really mean of the farm areas on the edges."

"Mm." A soft pattering of computer keys came through the phone. "Here's one. Done when the airport was extended, a few years back."

"No, wrong area." Sally's eagerness began seeping away. Was this another lead balloon? "How about on the southeast edge of town?"

"Let's see..." More pattering. "Well, here's something. But this one goes way back to the early 1950s. It was the first aerial survey ever done of Knollvale. The whole city was surveyed, and the surrounding rural areas as well. You wouldn't want that, I guess."

"As a matter of fact, it could be just what I'm looking for!" Sally's optimism flowed back. "What I'd really like to see are the original photographs taken for the survey. Would that be possible?" She held her breath.

"Uh... that far back?" He sounded doubtful. "We wouldn't keep them here, I don't think. Let me check." Another flurry of keys. "No. Sorry, they're long gone."

Sally groaned and slumped against the real estate office window.

"They'd be in Archives now."

She straightened up. "Archives! Where's that?"

"Top floor of this building. Got a pencil handy? Here's the date

125

and index number of the survey."

She pulled her notebook from her bag and jotted the numbers down, then thanked the man wholeheartedly. After thumbing off, she phoned Jones & Hewens to let Fay know where she could be found in the next hour or so.

"Ermine's been up and down those stairs a dozen times already," Fay muttered. Sally guessed she didn't want to be overheard. "I don't know if you'll be able to search her apartment today. Maybe I could do it, if I can grab a chance."

"I don't want you taking any risks."

"Sally, I'm not dumb. I wouldn't try it unless she was clear out of the way."

"Just be careful!"

WITH THE HELP of an Archives technician, Sally outlined the area she was interested in on a grid-covered map. "Find a table to yourself," the woman said cheerfully. "You'll need the space."

She came back a few minutes later wheeling a cartload of cardboard boxes. Pulling out a sheaf of black-and-white photographs, she flipped one over to show a number pencilled on the back.

"That's the key to laying them out. And, see the pinholes? You line these up..." She demonstrated. "That shows you how much to overlap the photos." She left her to it.

Sally was fascinated to see a landscape spreading over the table as she laid the photographs out in overlapping rows. It was like riding in the survey plane as it flew back and forth across the countryside.

But it wasn't much use unless she could find the area she wanted. She put the pictures back in their box, then opened the next. Still nothing but trees and fields, broken by fence lines and roads. Nothing to show what property she was looking at.

In the fifth box she found roofs. This could be it! Sally's pulse quickened as she laid out the pictures. This batch gave her a top view of a farmhouse with a row of sheds nearby. A narrow road curved in close to the house. The shapes and the pattern they made together looked exactly like the buildings on Ermine's property.

But the grounds looked different in these photos: more open and bare. Sally frowned at this, until she realized the woods around the studio must have grown up since the property stopped being a working farm. That could easily have happened in the past sixty years.

Now, where was the barn? She carefully eased the raft of pictures along the table and started laying out the contents of the next box. They matched along the bottom edge of the first batch.

And here, finally, was the barn. Its roof looked solid, and a big fenced yard surrounded it. Sally focused on the area between the barn and the house.

Here was where she'd left the car. Her finger moved slowly across the black-and-white panorama. *Here* she'd looked at the barn, and started walking toward it through the woods. Only, in this photo the woods were a meadow dotted with only a few trees. Other than that, there was nothing to see.

Or wasn't there? She bent lower, squinting. Behind her, someone said, "Here, try this." Sally looked up to see the technician holding out a magnifying glass.

"Thanks! Just what I need." She moved the glass over the picture and fine detail leaped up at her.

The woman laughed. "What are you searching for, buried treasure?"

"In a way, yes." Then she held the glass still. For a moment she didn't dare breathe. "And I think... I may have just found it."

Chapter 35

Trap

SALLY TOOK OUT her notebook and sketched a rough map, adding the photo's reference number in case it needed to be checked later. Then hastily shuffled the pictures into order and slid them into their boxes.

Her heart was beating double-quick with excitement. *I've got to tell Fay and Tasha about this!* She got up from the table and pulled her cellphone from her pocket. As she was thumbing it on, the helpful technician crossed the floor.

"Excuse me? We ask that all cellphones be kept off in the Archives. Out of consideration for others." She nodded at a sign on the wall. "I should have pointed that out: sorry."

"But — oh, okay. I'm just leaving anyway. Thanks a million for all your help!" Sally shoved the phone into her bag with the notebook and pen.

"Actually, I came over to tell you there's a call for you at the service desk."

"Call for me here? Who is it?"

"Don't know." The woman smiled. "But it sounds like life and death!"

It was Fay, breathless with excitement. "She's gone!"

"Who?" But Sally guessed who, and her hand tightened on the receiver.

"Ermine! About ten minutes ago she went out, saying she was going shopping. Soon as she was out of sight I sneaked upstairs and

128

— guess what?"

"She'd cleared out."

"Everything! All her clothes, her personal stuff — gone! And the fireplace was full of ashes. It looked like she'd been burning paper."

"And I bet I know where she's heading." Sally set her teeth. There was no time to describe what she'd found in the survey photos. "Fay, will you do one more thing?"

"Name it."

"Phone Detective Braun and get him to meet me at the airport. Tell him Ermine's skipping out and we have the proof he needs to arrest her. Say I'll be in the terminal, near the entrance."

Sally hung up, shouldered her bag and ran to the stairs, too impatient to wait for the elevator. Minutes later the Honda was threading through busy streets toward the highway, the quickest route to the airport.

As she accelerated up the entry ramp, excitement flooded through her. After so many dead ends, she was nearly at the end of this maze!

Then a noise behind her made her look up. A rustling sound in the back seat, like a loose box sliding back and forth. But there wasn't any...

In the rearview mirror, a pair of icy grey eyes met hers. They narrowed in a malicious smile. Beside them rose a second, heavier, redder face.

Alys giggled. "Didn't I tell you to keep looking over your shoulder? Man, Sally, did you get careless!"

"Very, very careless, Sally Sharp." Dylan smiled his sly, tight-lipped smile.

Alys giggled again. "Some detective! Can't even detect two extra passengers in the back seat."

"What happened, Dylan?" Sally asked lightly. "Did Eddie run

away with the Corvette? Or did your parents finally ground you?"

At once she was sorry for baiting him. In the rearview mirror Dylan's face twisted with fury. This was not the way to handle him.

It wasn't the place she would have chosen for this head-to-head, either. Not on a high-speed highway at rush hour, surrounded by other cars, all going over the speed limit. There was zero room for mistakes.

"I owe you a whole lot of aggravation," Dylan snarled in her ear. "And now you're going to get it back. All of it."

"Okay, let's talk about it. Not here, though. Soon as I get off this highway..."

"Shut it!" Alys hissed. "You turned me in to the cops, you sneak. I said I'd get you for it and I will."

"Be smart, Alys. Up till now you've only been charged with theft." Sally's sweaty hands slipped on the wheel and her stomach was a lump of ice, but she kept her voice calm and reasonable. "I don't think you really want to make things any worse for yourself."

"How would you know what I want? Or what I could do? I can do anything I like!"

Something cold and hard pressed against the side of her neck. Reflected in the mirror, it gleamed. Sally stiffened. Alys laughed gloatingly.

"That's right, drive carefully. I'd hate to cut your throat... by accident, anyway."

"I don't think you'd want to do that on purpose either, not at this speed." Sally produced a laugh. "Think what would happen if I were to swerve just now."

As if to underline her meaning, a transport truck thundered by. It seemed to pass within inches.

Dylan cursed. "Give me the knife, Alys. I know how to use it, you don't."

"No! I—"

"Give me the knife!"

Sulkily, Alys handed it over. In Dylan's thick-fingered hand it still hovered too close to Sally's neck, but she felt a degree safer.

Even now she couldn't stop being a detective. It struck her that Alys and Dylan were both in a hyped-up, overconfident state of mind and probably thought they had nothing to lose: Alys especially. Maybe they'd be cocky enough to spill some information.

"Thanks, Dylan," she said coolly. "You're right not to trust her with a weapon. You never know when she'll turn on you. She's a killer, that one."

"Killer?" Alys burst out. "That's a lie!"

"You killed Mrs. Mahon, right?" Sally faked a careless shrug, not easy while watching the road and the traffic. "When she caught you stealing."

"Are you ever off base! That was Ermine. I just helped her fake the burglary."

"I don't believe you. Why should you've helped her? What could be in it for you?"

"Eight hundred bucks, that's what." Alys sounded smug. "And there'll be more before I'm finished with her. Lots more!"

Sally's mouth tightened. So that was where the gold watch and the expensive outfits came from. Blackmail, just as she'd suspected.

More important, she knew for sure that Alys was a key witness. Now, if only she could talk her way out of this situation, and talk Alys into telling what she knew...

"Now you've done it, stupid!" Dylan said heavily. "She knows too much. We'll have to get rid of her."

"Don't be so antsy! All we have to do is lean on her. Scare her a little."

"I've tried that and it's no good. She's too stupid to scare. No, we'll have to fix her and it has to be permanent."

Sally went cold as she realized what he was saying. His "permanent fix" meant murder.

Chapter 36

Weapon on Wheels

SOMEHOW SHE KEPT her mind on the driving, watching for signs, signalling lane changes, keeping up to speed.

The turnoff to the airport would soon be coming up. Off to her right she glimpsed the flat expanse of the runways. Two or three planes sat there like big white gulls in a field, while another scudded in low, preparing to land.

"Pass the next exit," Dylan said. "Take the next after that."

"But there's nothing out there but woods," Alys protested.

Dylan's eyes met Sally's in the mirror. They crinkled with laughter. "That'll suit us just fine," he said silkily.

Ahead loomed an overhead sign. KNOLLVALE AIRPORT NEXT EXIT – KEEP RIGHT. Sally gripped the wheel firmly and breathed deeply, evenly. She'd been in tight spots before and found a way out. She'd find her way out of this one.

She wasn't unarmed, either. In its way, the modest little Honda Civic was a weapon far more powerful than Dylan's knife.

He held the blade up now so that it flashed at her in the rearview mirror. "Remember." He showed his teeth. "Do as you're told, and you *might* make it out alive."

"I have a better plan," she said calmly. With a twist of the wheel she veered into the right lane.

"What are you doing?" Dylan yelped. "You heard what I said!" The cold threat of the knife blade was against her neck again. "Get out of this!"

"Too late." Sally took the curving exit ramp faster than she liked. But she was still fully in control of the car. Once on the straight, heading for the airport, she put her foot down on the accelerator and the Honda leaped ahead.

Alys was screaming threats. "Keep it cool," Sally shouted gaily over her shoulder. "You wouldn't want to distract me now!"

The Honda shot past the car ahead, darted in front of an oncoming van, and shot around a corner with squealing tires. For a moment the wheel fought Sally's grip. Then she had it under control again.

Another corner. Dylan wasn't waving the knife now, just gripping the back of her seat with both hands and yelling. His reflected face looked white. Alys wasn't visible. Sally wondered briefly if she'd been thrown into a corner.

Two seconds later the car arrowed through a gate into the parking lot. Sally stamped on the brake. The car spun and bucked to a stop, and the two in the back piled up against one side.

Sally released her seatbelt with a slap and was out the door, all in one smooth lunge. She raced for the terminal's big glass entrance doors. Only when she was inside did she stop and turn, panting, to look back.

Dylan had climbed into the front seat of the Honda. Sally mentally kicked herself for leaving the keys in the ignition, but there hadn't been time to take them out. As she watched, the car took off with a roar.

"Good ol' Red," she said. "I sure hope they don't damage you!" But Dylan and Alys were a headache for the police now. She walked into the terminal to look for Ermine.

Chapter 37

Total Failure

THERE WAS NO sign of Detective Braun in the terminal building. No sign of Ermine, either. Sally's stomach lurched a little as it occurred to her for the first time that she might have been wrong. Suppose Ermine hadn't been heading to the airport after all?

On the other hand, perhaps she just hadn't arrived yet. Sally walked slowly across the echoing expanse, scanning people standing in queues and others who sat waiting for their flights. Then she caught sight of a sign on the far wall: FIRST CLASS LOUNGE.

The lounge doors were glass. Sally edged up to them and peered in, then smiled in satisfaction. Ermine was sitting in a comfortable chair, looking trim in a fitted cherry-red business suit. She turned the pages of a copy of *Vogue*, her expression relaxed and confident.

As Sally watched, a speaker pinged and began blaring announcements. Ermine lifted her head to listen. "Passengers to Mexico City," the brassy voice said. "Flight 103 will board in thirty minutes from exit B." Ermine nodded, and returned to her magazine.

Sally strode across the room to the reservations desk and looked at the monitor above the clerk's head. Times of departures and arrivals scrolled slowly down. Flight 103 was due to take off in fifty-five minutes.

She paced impatiently. Where was Braun? Maybe Fay hadn't been able to get through to him. Or maybe, she thought with a sinking feeling, Fay hadn't been able to convince him. Braun wasn't exactly on good terms with Sally or her friends just now.

Whatever, she had to try again. She reached for her cellphone, and found — an empty pocket. The phone wasn't in her other pocket, either. It must have fallen out in her leap from the car. It might still be lying in the parking lot, unharmed, if she was lucky. She headed for the doors. Halfway there she skidded to a halt.

Not the parking lot. Her phone was in her car, which was now probably miles away. She could picture herself in the Archives, stuffing the phone into her bag. Then slinging the bag onto the front passenger seat of the Honda.

Okay — public phone booth! She whirled, searching with her eyes, and spotted a row of booths on the opposite side of the main lounge. It wasn't until she'd arrived there, breathless, and picked up the receiver, that she realized she had no money. Her change purse was also in her bag, which was in the Honda, which was now miles away.

Please.... please... Desperately, Sally dug in her front jeans pockets. "Pay dirt!" There was a quarter in one pocket, a dime in the other. But that wasn't enough. She tried the back pockets and came up with a crumpled Kleenex and a wintergreen mint.

Biting her lip, she thought feverishly. Then darted out of the booth and into the next one. Sometimes people forgot to collect their change from the coin return. She poked a finger into the slot. Nope.

Next booth; try again. Yes! She found a dime and added it to the coins clenched in her left fist. Now she was only a nickel short.

Next booth: no luck. Sally resisted the urge to tear her hair out with both hands. She looked around the terminal at the dozens, maybe hundreds of busy people, and wondered...

She had never begged. She wasn't sure she could bring herself to do it.

And wasn't there some rule against panhandling in the airport?

Maybe she'd just get herself thrown out. Was it worth the risk?

She noticed a kind-looking woman wearing a clerical collar who was sitting in the open lounge area nearby. She was just nerving herself up to cross the floor and speak, when a tap on the shoulder spun her around.

A security guard stood there: a grim-faced man with a bristling grey moustache. "Problem?" His voice was a bark. His eyes were flinty.

"No! Not at all." She started backing away.

"You sure? Looked to me like you were scrounging for change."

"Well..."

"You need to make a phone call?"

Sally pulled herself together. "Yes. I'm just a little short."

"Okay, here." He dug in a pocket and held out a handful of loonies and quarters.

Her mouth opened wide, then snapped shut. *Wow, you really can't tell a book by its cover!* She took a breath. "All I need is another five cents." She showed her own handful of change.

"Just a nickel?"

"Just a nickel."

The guard's eyebrows flicked up and a smile came into the hard eyes. He picked up a coin and dropped it on her palm. "There you go. Live large, eh?"

"Thanks!" She flashed him a brilliant smile, dashed back to the payphones, fed in the coins and punched in the number, which by now she knew by heart.

The receiver clicked and a voice growled in her ear. "Braun. Homicide."

"Please listen," Sally said urgently. "This is Sally Sharp. I'm at the airport, and so is Ermine Jones. She's about to leave for—"

"That's the limit! I'm fed up with you, Miss. Now, get off the line and let me get back to work!"

"Wait! Don't you dare hang up! Not till you've heard me out. Remember you said you owed me one for helping you catch Alys? Well, now I'm collecting."

There was a silence, then a heavy sigh. "All right. I'll listen just once more. But don't push your luck."

"I won't. I'm offering you a chance to catch the person who killed Kendra Mahon and attacked Mrs. Engstrom and kidnapped Valerie."

"And who might that be?"

"Ermine Jones."

"You've got a motive? Proof? Witnesses?"

"Yes, yes and yes. Motive: Ermine stole Kendra's fashion designs and got caught. She killed Kendra to keep from being ruined. I have solid evidence of the plagiarism. And I have a witness who knows about the murder and helped Ermine fake a burglary to cover it up."

"Izzat so." He sounded as if he was doing something else: reading his email, maybe. "So, who's this witness?"

"Alys Krug. Right now she and Dylan Thatcher are driving my red Honda Civic. Here's the license number." She gave it. "They tried to hijack me, so you can add attempted kidnapping and car theft — at knifepoint — to the list of charges against them. Oh, and Alys is also a blackmailer. She was extorting money from Ermine. I think that gives you enough leverage. I'm sure she'll talk, if you handle her right."

He made a growling sound. "You've been busy lately, haven't you, Sally? Got any other advice for me?"

She hesitated. "Just that I think I may know where Valerie

138

Hewens is being held. As soon as we find her, Peter will speak up about Ermine. He'll be your key witness."

"So you've got it all sewn up!" Braun said sarcastically. "You don't need the police, Sally. Why don't you just arrest the perp yourself and throw her in jail?"

Sally frowned at the graffiti-scratched acrylic panel in front of her eyes. What was wrong with him? Why was he reacting like this?

"Okay, that's it." His voice changed. "I've heard you out and now I figure I've been patient long enough."

She was shocked. "Don't you believe me?"

"Frankly, no. Why should I? Almost every time you've come barreling into this case, you've wasted my time. We searched the Jones lady's property and turned up no sign of any crime."

"But—"

He steamrollered her. "You've wasted valuable police time and manpower once too often. If you do it again, Sally, I'll have you charged with public mischief. Is that understood?"

There was no use trying to argue. "Yes!" she snapped back. "But you're making a horrible mistake!"

The line went dead.

Chapter 38

Last Chance

SALLY GLARED at the receiver, strangled the impulse to bash something with it, and quietly hung up.

She checked the time display. Ermine's plane was due to take off in just under forty minutes. She stepped out of the booth and looked around for the surprisingly nice security guard. No sign of him.

Super. Sally lifted her arms and let them drop. She had no phone, no money, no ID, no car, and no way to stop a killer from going free.

"Sal! Over here!"

She swung around and laughed with relief. Tasha came trotting across the room toward her, waving. Sally ran to meet her.

"Fay couldn't get Braun to listen to her," Tasha said. "Or Peter either. So she got hold of me. She thought you might need help."

"You bet I do." Sally nodded at the glass door of the first class lounge. "Ermine's in there waiting for her flight. Unless we can pull off a miracle in the next half-hour, we've lost her."

Tasha made a face. "I don't know what we can do. She doesn't have any other properties, I found that out, anyway. Where could Val be?"

"I'm certain she's being held on the farm." Sally grabbed Tasha's arm and strode at top speed toward the exit. "It's a long shot that we'll find her in the next thirty minutes, but it's the only shot we've got."

"But the farm's been searched!"

"Not all of it. Come on. We're almost out of time!"

As they took the quickest route back to the studio, Sally told Tasha what had led her to check the survey photos, and what she'd seen in them.

"If I can just locate the spot... Oh, no!" She groaned.

"What now?"

"I sketched a map. Big help! It's in my bag, which is in my car." She thumped a fist on her leg in frustration. "I'll have to rely on memory."

"There are four of us, counting Peter. We'll all search. Maybe we can get some of the studio workers to help too." Tasha slowed down to make the turn into the Jones & Hewens driveway.

"It's getting late. They'll have gone home by now." Sally checked the time display on the dashboard yet again. Her heart sank. Just over fifteen minutes were left until Ermine's plane was scheduled to take off. *We're not going to make it.*

Then she lifted her chin and squared her shoulders. *Oh, yes, we are!* The moment the car came to a stop she ducked out and raced to the front door of the farmhouse.

Fay came to meet her. "Sal! I'm so glad Tasha found you. I couldn't make that awful man take me seriously!"

"Neither could I. Where's Peter?"

"In his office. Everyone else has gone home."

With Fay and Tasha close behind, Sally ran along the hall and into the workroom. Without the clatter of sewing machines and the buzz of voices, the big room felt abandoned and cold.

Peter's office door was closed. Sally tapped on the panel and went in without waiting for an answer. Fay and Tasha stood in the doorway. Peter was sitting behind his desk with his cellphone in front of him. He looked up as she came in, but said nothing.

"She's not going to call," Sally told him. "Trust me. She's going to fly away and let Val die."

"I don't believe it." His fists knotted on the desk.

"You have two choices," she said bluntly. "Sit there and wait — for nothing. Or come with me now and help me find Val. Before Ermine goes free."

"What are you talking about?"

"Val's here! I'm sure of it. Remember that time two days ago, when I heard her voice in the woods? And everybody thought it was my imagination?"

"Now you're saying it wasn't?" Peter looked away. "Sally, don't you know when to quit?"

Adrenaline and frustration bubbled in Sally's veins. She bit back a sharp answer. Any more argument was a waste of precious time. "Make up your mind!" she snapped.

She turned and ran from the office and from the workroom. Fay and Tasha raced at her heels. One after the other, the three girls shot out at the front door, then streamed around the house to the back.

Sally stopped in the spot where she'd parked Tasha's car two days ago, under the silver birch. It was the same time of the afternoon, which helped. Closing her eyes, she tried to picture exactly what she'd done the last time.

She opened her eyes and turned to face the barn. Slowly, fighting the urge to hurry, she pushed toward it through the rustling shrubbery.

"It was about here. I think." She turned to look back at the house. Had she come this far the last time? As she looked, a tall figure came running through the trees.

Peter came to a breathless halt at Sally's side. "What are we looking for?"

"In the photo it looked like a building of some kind. Square and small. A shed, maybe."

Fay gazed about through the trees, shaking her head.

"There's nothing here at all," Tasha said flatly. "It must have been torn down. Sixty years is a long time."

"There was something different about it." Sally paced slowly across the forest floor, scuffing her feet through the deep layer of dried leaves and humus. "It must've been quite short. It cast hardly any shadow, even though the sheds near the house cast really long shadows."

"What kind of structure could that be?" Peter kept pace with Sally, about a yard distant. Tasha and Fay ranged out on the other side of her. Together they covered a wide strip of ground.

"It doesn't sound like a shed," Fay commented. She stopped to kick a piece of half- rotted wood out of her way. "More like a hatch of some kind."

"Hatch?" Tasha asked.

"Yes. You know. Like a trap door, or a cellar lid. Something just a couple of inches tall."

Sally had stopped thinking about the time. If Ermine hadn't taken off by now, she couldn't have more than a few minutes to wait. The important thing now was to find Valerie.

The toe of her sneaker kicked out another piece of mouldering wood. She stooped to pick it up.

"Wait. Look at this!" The piece was straight and smooth, where it wasn't rotted. Not a fallen branch.

Peter ran a hand over it. "That's been shaped by tools. And see there? A nail hole." His face glowed with excitement. "This could be it!"

143

Chapter 39

Look Up, Look Down

"YES, IT COULD BE a part of the square thing in the picture." Sally tried hard not to get carried away. "Or it might have nothing at all to do with it."

"I kicked up a bit of that just a second ago!" Fay began shuffling enthusiastically back and forth through the debris, and Tasha joined her. Dry leaves flew up into the air.

Peter turned around in all directions. He made a trumpet with his hands and shouted: "Valerie! Where are you?"

"Wait!" Sally hissed. "Sh! I thought I heard something."

Silence fell. She strained to pick up that sound again, but all she heard was her own heartbeat thudding in her ears. Peter walked across to stand beside her. Tasha and Fay froze in place, listening.

There! A thin, distant thread of a voice. Then it was gone. "Did you hear that?" Sally demanded.

Peter shook his head. "Not me," Fay said. "Maybe it was the wind."

"Peter, call her name again." Sally turned to him urgently. "No, wait. Let's all call together. Come on, loud as we can! One... two... three..."

"Valerie!"

A long silence. A wind stirred the trees. A crow cawed. Fay started to say something and Tasha caught her arm to silence her. Then...

They all heard it this time.

Peter... help... help...

"Val!" Peter gasped. "But where is she? It sounds like she's calling from a million miles away!"

"She couldn't be up a tree, could she?" Tasha peered up into the treetops.

Sally laughed. "Look down instead of up, Tash!" As she spoke she dropped to her knees in the place where she'd kicked up the piece of wood. The others knelt beside her. Four pairs of hands dug into the carpet of dry leaves. Below that was thick black humus.

Suddenly Sally's nails scraped a soft woody surface with a hard core under it. She brushed away more humus and found a plank laid flat to the ground.

"Looks like Fay was right," Peter muttered. He hurled dirt and leaves away in handfuls. "This has to be a trap door."

"Out in the woods?" Tasha asked. "What for?"

Sally pushed hair out of her eyes with a grimy hand. "Sixty years ago this was an open meadow. And, halfway between the house and the barn — what better place for a storm cellar?"

They cleared a wooden shape about two feet square, set inside a frame of crumbling planks. Peter got his fingers under one edge of the square and heaved. It came up with a shower of dead leaves and fell with a thud onto the ground nearby.

Where the wood had been they found a square of darkness. A cold, earthy, damp smell wafted up from below. At first Sally could see nothing. Then, as her eyes adapted to the dark, she saw something huddled in a corner, perhaps three yards below.

A white oval turned up to them. It was Valerie's face, wet with tears.

Chapter 40

The Day After

"I WISH I'D been sitting beside Ermine at the moment she realized." Peter smiled with savage satisfaction. "I wish I'd seen the look on her face when the plane slowed down and stopped instead of taking off. For once, she didn't have things all her own way."

"It was close, though," Sally said. "Two minutes is not a lot of leeway. It's a good thing R.J. Braun can move fast, once he does decide to move."

Morning sunshine flooded in through the windows of the hospital room. After nearly a week in the dark, Valerie's eyes still weren't comfortable with strong light, but she flatly refused to have the curtains closed.

It was Friday morning, the day after Ermine's arrest. Sally had come to visit Val and report on her meeting with Detective Braun.

Fay and Tasha had come with her. They had filled a vase with pink and blue asters and set shopping bags full of paperback books and magazines beside Valerie's bed. Also in the bags were an iPod with headphones, and packets of chocolates, nuts and fruit jellies.

"You're all so good to me." Valerie looked around at them happily. "As soon as my stomach gets back to normal, I'm going to pig out! On anything except apples," she added with a shudder. "I'll never touch another apple so long as I live!"

A small bag of apples and two half-litre bottles of water had been all she'd had to eat or drink in the storm cellar where Ermine had put her. After four days the supplies had run out, although Valerie had

146

tried to make them last.

The medics had found her weak, dehydrated and badly chilled. She wasn't hurt otherwise, although they said the emotional scars might take longer to heal.

"You got your car back, Sally?" Peter asked now.

"Uh-huh. Alys and Dylan didn't get far. And when Alys learned of the string of charges against her — and found out she wasn't going to make any more money off Ermine — she decided to testify, just as we'd hoped she would."

"I hope Ermine gets locked up for a good long time," Peter said fiercely.

"She will, thanks to you and Val. Especially Val." Sally smiled at her.

Valerie shivered and pulled the pink hospital blanket up around her shoulders. "I don't think I'll ever forget the expression on her face, when I woke up at the bottom of that hole and saw her pulling the ladder up. She looked at me as if I were some kind of a bug. Not a person at all."

Ermine had kidnapped Valerie by the simple method of visiting her at home, knocking her on the head and dragging her out to the car on a blanket. The neighbours had seen nothing through the screen of shrubbery.

Mrs. Engstrom had been mugged to keep her from witnessing the kidnapping, but the attack also provided a plausible reason for Valerie's "running off."

Luckily the old lady's hard head and tough constitution had kept her alive. She was out of the coma now, and was expected to recover completely within a few weeks. Since they were in the same hospital, Valerie had already been able to pay her a visit.

As Braun had hoped, Mrs. Engstrom had caught a glimpse of her attacker. The description fitted Ermine Jones.

"Almost the worst thing was always being in the dark." Valerie shivered again, and Peter reached for her hand. "She left a flashlight, but the batteries gave out in an hour or so. But the *very* worst thing was — I was just so darn scared! I thought — I thought I would never — And, and things would crawl in and—"

Seeing that Val was about to fall apart again, Sally sat on the bed beside her and slipped an arm around her shoulders. "Everything's okay now," she murmured. "You're out of there. It's over."

"I thought I'd never get out!" Val gulped. "Then one time, I heard footsteps on the hatch overhead, and I yelled and yelled, and nobody answered. I thought it must be Ermine. I'd have been glad even to see her!"

"It was me." Sally looked at her guiltily. "If only I'd stopped and tried to pinpoint the sound, instead of rushing off the way I did! You might have been free three days ago."

"Never mind, Sally." Peter reached across and clasped her hand. "It was you who found her in the end. You just wouldn't give up looking, even when everybody was on your back to stop. Including me," he added darkly.

"Sally," Val said softly, "you saved my life."

Sally flushed and gave her a hug. "Me and a whole bunch of other people."

"But if I hadn't asked your help in the first place..." She sighed and snuggled down among the blankets. "Could sleep now... so tired..."

They tiptoed out. As they walked down the corridor toward the elevators, Fay managed to end up at Peter's side. "What now?" she asked brightly. "For Jones & Hewens, I mean. The partnership's over, I'd guess."

"Of course." He stuck his hands in his pockets and his dark eyes flashed with determination. "I'm on my own. And that's the way it's going to stay. No more partnerships, nothing borrowed or second hand. Just me."

"Does that mean the retro look is out?" Sally asked.

"For me it is. I'm going to launch out again in my own place, using strictly original designs. No more Corduroy Rose! I'll have a new label, a new look — a new start."

The elevator opened and they crowded in. Fay tapped the ground-floor button. "Will your new place be in town, or are you taking over the farmhouse?"

"Neither. I'm going back to Toronto."

Fay clapped her hands to her mouth. "Oh no!"

The elevator doors slid open and they walked out into the lobby. All except Fay, who was so stunned that she just stood there. Tasha had to reach back in and pull her out of the elevator before the doors closed.

"That's too bad," Sally said, as they crossed the lobby to the revolving doors. "But I guess I can see why."

Peter nodded at her. "Knollvale hasn't been good for Val or me. I think we both need to move on."

One by one they circled through the doors and out. Together they headed toward the parking lot.

"You won't see much of me from now on," Peter said as they stopped beside Sally's car. "I have a ton of work and planning to do."

"So this is goodbye?" said Fay in a small voice.

"Not quite! There's just one thing I've made up my mind about. First thing I'll do, I'm going to design an original outfit for each of you, and I'll have them cut and sewn up. You'll have them before the start of school." He shared a dazzling smile around. "My way of saying thanks."

Then he was on his way, with another smile and a wave. They watched him climb into the yellow Mustang, pull out and disappear into traffic.

Chapter 41

Power of Three

"A PETER HEWENS original designed just for me!" Fay was breathless, her hand on her heart. "Oh, how I'll flaunt it! That almost makes up for this being the end of my fabulous career in the fashion industry."

"Fabulous, huh?" Tasha circled around the car to the passenger's side. They were all travelling in Sally's Honda today to save on fuel costs, since none of them had a job any more. "I'd describe my career in the fashion industry as just plain boring. I'm glad it's over. What about you, Sal?"

Sally checked to make sure everybody was in and belted, then keyed the ignition. "Me? Short and painful, I'd describe it." She touched her forehead, where the bruise from being pushed downstairs showed mottled green and purple. "But an eye-opener, for sure. I learned a lot, and that's always good."

"One thing I learned," Fay said as they left the parking lot, "no matter what you're doing, if you want to succeed there's one thing you absolutely need to have."

"And what's that?" Sally asked.

"A catchy label!"

"A label! For us?" Tasha twisted around to stare. "What the heck for?"

"So people know what we're all about! So they take us seriously!" Fay bounced excitedly. "Like a fashion house, or a rock band, or a political party!"

"Us a rock band?" Tasha snickered.

"That's just an example. We three, we're a detective team, right? So let's think of a name. Why don't we call ourselves..." She rolled up her eyes to the car roof and waved her hands. "Oh... Triple Threat. How's that? Or Power of Three. Or Sally's Seekers. Or..."

Tasha whooped with laughter. "Or Sally's Sneakers!"

"That's just silly. Wait, how about this — *Safata*. That's our names all run together." Fay punched the air. "Yes! Doesn't that sound exotic and mysterious? *Safata*."

"Or, hey! Turn it around." Tasha chortled. "*Fatasa*. Sound it out. Fat—"

Sally laughed up at the sky through the windshield. It was a deep warm blue, but veiled along the horizon with a hint of autumn haze.

"Listen, you two. Let's go for a drive in the country before this gorgeous summer weather is all gone, okay? We'll find someplace nice to grab a bite and we'll eat outdoors. We'll sit in the sun and talk about everything. The future, and school, and clothes, and fun. And mystery, and danger, and exotic names."

And so they did.

About the author

PATRICIA BOW lives in Kitchener, Ontario. She has written more than twenty books for young people. To find out more about Patricia and her work, visit www.execulink.com/~thebows/patricia.htm.

www.ingramcontent.com/pod-product-compliance
Lightning Source LLC
Chambersburg PA
CBHW051244170626
46809CB00004B/1480